Imagine

Imagine

Robert Beane

Library of Congress Control Number:		2016905089
ISBN:	Hardcover	978-1-5144-8008-3
	Softcover	978-1-5144-8007-6
	eBook	978-1-5144-8006-9

Print information available on the last page.

Rev. date: 04/25/2016

To order additional copies of this book, contact:
Xlibris
1-888-795-4274
www.Xlibris.com
Orders@Xlibris.com
731835

PREFACE

Sometimes, in the small hours of the morning, when we are somewhere halfway between deep sleep, dreams, and waking up, then in those quiet moments, we are given gifts. The gift givers are different for each of us. And what we do with those gifts is a decision that we all make as individuals.

For me, this story came as a series of gifts. One little piece at a time. I am aware of the messages that I hear in the natural world: in my deep meditations, in that folk music that I love so much, in those certain songs that reach out and touch me strongly. One of those songs is this one.

Imagine

Imagine there's no countries, it isn't hard to do.
Nothing to kill or die for, no religion too.
Imagine all the people, living life in peace.
You! You may say I'm a dreamer
but I'm not the only one.
I hope someday you will join us
and the world will be as one.

—John Lennon (Oct. 9, 1940–Dec. 8, 1980)
(Released in 1971)

As you read this story, allow your imagination to exercise itself. You can dream of a world that is healed. Or you can dream of a world that is doomed to destruction. Or you may dream that this story is just fiction. For me, this story is a hope that some people will listen and try to make positive changes to this world that we share with so many other beings. We are not alone here. If we destroy the environment on this world, then all life here will die.

ACKNOWLEDGMENTS

There are so many people who have encouraged me to write. I can name but a few, but I owe them all for their support.

Bill Yates, who told me those fateful words: "Just remember, all those stories you have in your head, if you don't write them down on paper, when you are gone, so are they."

My Mary, my wife, my huckleberry. You who are the first person to hear these words as I set them down in ink.

Mary Snell, facilitator for the Writers Group, you have given me so much guidance.

Chris, Skip, Leanne, Dee, Terry, Linda, and Warren—those other members of the Writers Group who gave me my first encouragement.

Lee Heffner, your encouragement made me take that final step in this process: to step through that door marked Courage.

CHAPTER ONE

"Hello and welcome to you both. We have been waiting for you to arrive."

Joey's memories were always there at some level of his consciousness. Some of them, he never wanted to forget; some of them, he wished that he could forget. He had been born and raised in one of those old New England cities that had been the breeding grounds for despair for three hundred years, in an inner-city, working-class neighborhood where many languages were spoken and where they all said the same thing: "All ye who enter here, give up your hope. Hope has no place here." You were born; you grew to adulthood; you got married; you had kids; you lived in an apartment near your parents; you worked at some sort of labor-intensive job; you flushed your dreams away with alcohol; you died, and another generation stepped into your place. And if you lashed out at your family with violence, well, those around you would just nod in agreement, because they did the same thing.

Joey made a decision at an early point in his life to walk away from all of it. He wanted to make his own way in life. He kept feeling that there was something more for him, that it involved saving lives, not taking lives, that it involved striving for peace and a sense of inner peace. Joey became that strange kid in school who read a lot and was quiet and shy. He always seemed to be thinking things over. He would later understand that he was a true introvert. As a means of escaping the neighborhood, he went into the military, but he chose a lifesaving branch instead of one that taught you to shoot people. His thoughts were that he was fine with risking his life to save someone else but that he would not risk his life to kill someone else.

When his military commitment ended, he drifted into one of the public-safety fields that focused on lifesaving. At twenty-three years old, he was not sure what he wanted to do with his life. During one of his desperate attempts at reaching out to escape from where he was, he met Joanne. He would later figure out that he had married her not for herself but for where she had been born and raised, in a small town in the mountains of Western Maine. After two years of them both trying to make it work, the marriage died a quiet death. He stayed with it for an additional sixteen years, trying to save what was, in reality, already lying composting in a graveyard. But his efforts were not enough.

A close friend told him, "You are like the scientist who has a theory. He experiments and experiments to try to prove it and finally stops experimenting when his theory proves no good."

So he separated and filed for a divorce.

An ugly, vicious divorce later, and Joey was wandering again, trying to find his way in this life. He was retired now and taking a few classes in college. One day, listening to his intuition, he sought out a divorce support group, and there he met Leigh. It was love at first sight for them both. They dated for a while then tried living together for four years, and after getting used to each other, they married. It was now eleven years since their first meeting, and they were still devoted to each other.

Joey had, for many years, felt drawn toward the spiritual world of Buddhism and the native cultures from around the world. He didn't know why he was drawn to them, but he pursued the feelings that he was experiencing. He began to take classes in it all. He began to welcome that world of peace and serenity that he found there. He began to accept whatever changes were occurring within himself. He found himself becoming someone that other people sought out to help themselves heal from their hurts and with their journeys toward peace. He was becoming a magnet for those seeking help. His studies told him that he had become that peaceful man who had traveled through the life stages of warrior, teacher, healer, and sage.

Early summer in Maine can be a time of great beauty. The memories of the last winter were fading with the warmth of the growing season and the chance to stay outdoors without having to wear multiple layers of clothing to offset the bitter cold. Joey had been working hard at his chores around the house, but he had been feeling very strongly pulled to revisit an area that he hadn't thought of in many years. His intuition was once again yelling in his ear to take the time to take a drive up there. There, was the Eustis Maine, area, just sixteen miles from the Canadian border. Today was the day.

He told Leigh, "Hi, hon. I'm going to take a drive up to Eustis tomorrow. You have the day off from work. Would you like to go with me? We should be back in time for dinner."

Her reply was "Sure. That would be great to get out of Dodge for the day."

The next morning, they got into his pickup truck and headed out on to what used to be a very familiar route to the Western Mountains of Maine. His plan was to drive there, spend some time visiting and maybe meeting some old friends, and then return home before evening.

Leaving his home, he drove to Gray Village, and turning left onto Route 202, he headed for Lewiston. It was a beautiful, sunny, warm morning. Skirting the Lewiston downtown area by using the Airport Road, they connected with Route 4 and headed north. Shortly, they passed the Twitchell Airport. Staying on Route 4, they came to Livermore Falls. Crossing the Androscoggin River, they both felt again that gentle peace from that great River Spirit who lives in that river. Then entering the town, they took a short dogleg to the right and then to the left; they headed up and over that scenic Route 133. This beautiful stretch of road would, after about twenty miles, bring them to Farmington. This beautiful college town, home to the University of Maine, Farmington College, with its dorms and classrooms and its well-earned reputation for its teaching degree programs. Leaving here and heading north on Route 4, they passed the homestead of one of Maine's most respected state senators, Margaret Chase Smith. Now their trip would leave all the urban areas behind them.

Turning right onto Route 27 and starting the one-hour travel time to Eustis. Passing through the towns of New Vineyard; New Portland; and Kingfield, with its history of being the home of the Stanley brothers, who created the Stanley Steamer automobiles and its other favorite son who invented the earmuffs. Traveling northward through Carrabassett and into Stratton, with the first views of Flagstaff Lake and the north branch of the Dead River—Flagstaff Lake, with its history of completely submerging two towns when it was created as a hydrogeneration project in the 1930s—then finally into Eustis.

They stopped at the Pines convenience store for some take-out lunch, with plans to take it to the Alder Stream picnic area to eat it. Joey was remembering camping there often with friends years ago. As they left the Pines store, he was telling Leigh about the large truck-brake marks that were liberally scattered on the road surface, "Hon, do you see those marks on the road?"

"Yes."

"Hon, those marks are from tractor-trailer trucks locking up their brakes because of moose in the roadways."

As he was saying this, they drove over the crest of a small hill, and he had to step on the brakes hard. There was a large bull moose walking across the roadside in front of them. A short distance later, Joey turned off the road to the left and onto an old dirt roadway. A few hundred yards later, they stopped at the old picnic area at Alder Stream, with its outhouse, picnic table, and large fireplace.

Finding a place to sit at the picnic table and enjoy their lunch was easy. They were the only people at the picnic area. And the view of Alder Stream was quiet and serene.

"Hon, I have so many memories of this spot. Some of them great ones, and some of them painful ones. I camped here for over twelve years."

"I remember you talking about it."

They were sitting quietly and leaning against each other, when they heard sounds of someone walking toward them. Turning, they saw three men walking toward them from the direction of an old logging road that wove off into the forest toward their left. One of the men motioned to the others to follow him, and he walked to where Joey and Leigh were now standing. The man smiled and seemed to be relieved that he had found them.

The man said, "Are you Joey? And is this Leigh?"

Joey quietly answered, "Yes. But how do you know? And who are you?"

The man spoke again in a friendly voice, "I'm Arnor, and these are my friends, Josa and Bara. Please don't be frightened, Joey, We have been waiting for you to arrive here. We knew that you were coming here today. Can we sit with you and talk for a bit?"

Joey, very puzzled, very curious, and a bit on guard, motioned for them to sit down at the old picnic table that he and Leigh were sitting at. They looked all right, tall, trim, fit, and clean. He thought that they had a slight air of the military about themselves. He noticed other little things that seemed a little odd about them though. In the bright sunlight, their skin had a bluish tinge. Their hair had a very dark-blue tint. All three of them had dark-blue eyes. Their clothing seemed to be a sort of jumpsuit. He didn't recognize the fabric. He saw that each of them had some sort of a small medallion device attached to the right-side collar of their jumpsuit and that each medallion was different. Each one of them had on a cloth belt, buckled, with a few items attached to it. He was reminded of watching *Star Trek* when he was a child.

Arnor was watching Joey give them a studied look over. He chuckled a little.

"Please! Don't worry, Joey. We mean you no harm. And we have been waiting for you to arrive."

Joey reached over and put his arm protectively around Leigh, thinking to himself, *OK. How do I handle this one? And what can I do if they threaten us?*

CHAPTER TWO

Joey, looking at the leader intently, said again, "Who are you men? And what do you want?"

Arnor, still smiling, began to speak.

"Joey. I am our captain, and these men are part of my crew. We have been aware of you and Leigh, what you two are and have become for a very long time. We are not from this world. Our race travels between many worlds, and we watch them for certain signs of their evolving species. We have been watching this world and its humans for a very long time."

Bara spoke up and said, "Joey, I am our doctor/healer. There are humanoidlike beings on many worlds. We watch how they are evolving and if they are evolving. When they evolve to a certain point, we contact them and speak to them to help guide them."

Josa added in, "I am our ship's engineer. We have technology that allows us to travel through both time and space. We have visited here many times in this world's past."

Arnor spoke up again, "We contacted other humans on this world in the past and coached them in how to change how they thought about some things to help them with their process of evolving. We then tracked those humans to see how they affected others around themselves. You may be familiar with some of their names. They taught others to think in terms of peace and of nonviolence."

Joey blurted out, "But what has all of that got to do with us?"

Bara answered him, "Joey, we have watched you for some time. We have seen how you worked to overcome your childhood violence and abuse. You have worked to become a man of peace and someone who reaches out to help other people to heal themselves. Joey, you have unknowingly taken certain steps that have raised you up in the evolutionary process that Earth humans are just starting to become aware of. You are one of those humans who are standing on that leading edge of those Earth humans who are evolving to their next level of lightness. You are like the others that we contacted in this world's past."

Arnor spoke up, "Joey, one of those others was known as Sananda, who was also named Jesus. Another was the man known as the Buddha. Another was a woman known as Mother Theresa. There was also a man known as Gandhi."

Bara added in, "There have been others: the man known as Mandela and the man known as Martin Luther King."

Josa spoke, "Don't forget the man who wrote the songs about peace and brotherly love, John Lennon."

Bara added another familiar name to the list when he said, "And Mother Mary, who taught the man named Jesus."

Arnor added still more names, "The man named Da Vinci and the man named Einstein. Joey, they all worked for peace and progress toward universal brotherhood. We had spoken to them all."

Joey was stunned. His thoughts were in such a whirlwind. These names were a litany of some of his personal heroes. Now he was being told that they had been guided by beings from outside of this world. Added to his confusion was that this conversation was taking place at a picnic table while sitting in the sunshine, a few miles outside of Eustis, Maine, on a beautiful, early-summer day. During the last part of this conversation, Leigh had reached for his hand and was holding onto it so tightly that he was almost uncomfortable with it.

There was silence now. The initial flooding of words and thoughts had stopped for a moment like a wave receding at the seashore. Everyone seemed to be waiting for what was next.

Joey finally spoke up, "I don't know what to say. I still don't understand. Why are you here looking for me? I'm nobody. I'm just another guy working my way through things. Why are you here waiting for me?"

Arnor looked at Bara and Josa for a long moment, almost as if they were carrying on a rapid conversation by mental telepathy. They all finally nodded their heads in agreement. He turned back to Joey and said, "Leigh, you are an important part in this also, and we are very grateful to see you here. Joey, we would like to ask you both if you would like to join us for a trip."

Joey blurted out, "We can't leave here for a long trip. By the time we get back, we won't even be remembered by people."

Bara answered him by saying, "Joey, after we talked to your human scientist, Einstein, he was able to tell people that 'time is an illusion created by man'! He was right. If you come with us, we can return you to this time and to this place within a few hours of when, as you count time, you leave here."

Arnor said, "Joey, we hope that if you come with us, you can see other worlds! Some of them have known only peace, while others have followed the path that some humans here are following: that path toward self-destruction from violence. Perhaps if you see these differences, you can return and tell others. And your Earth human species can learn and take that next step upwards in their evolution."

Leigh looked at Joey, and still holding his hand tightly, she spoke to him, "This feels right. Let's go with them. Think about what we might learn from all of this."

Joey swallowed hard and took a deep breath, letting it out with a whoosh. He looked at Arnor and said, "OK! I trust you. We'll go with you. When do you want to leave? Can we finish our lunch first? Do we need to pack any clothes? What about food for us? Should I bring the keys to my truck? Should I leave a note on my dashboard? What about taking a shower? OK, OK, OK! Let's get going."

Arnor, Bara, and Josa were chuckling.

"Joey, we are used to you Earth humans! Don't worry. We have what you need on board our vessel. Please remember that all of us are some version of humans."

Taking a deep breath, Joey stepped back from the picnic table. He and Leigh walked around the table to join Arnor. Joey suddenly stopped. He turned and walked back to the table. He began to pick up the leftovers from their meal; Leigh helped him. They both took their picnic things to the truck, and putting them inside, Joey locked the truck and put the key in his pocket. The trash they both put into the rubbish barrel nearby. They both then looked at each other, and saying a polite excuse to the others, they each went to the outhouse nearby.

"It was one of those famous little houses out back, with the half-moon carved into the door, wooden buildings."

Once they were finished with that chore, they rejoined Arnor and his crew. With Arnor leading the way, they all started to walk toward the old logging road.

As the group walked along the old road, Arnor spoke to Joey, "How are your dreams doing, Joey?"

Joey stopped in his tracks, and turning his head, he looked at him. "What do you mean? How do you know about my dreams? My dreams are fine. What do you mean?"

Arnor slowed down his walking and waited for him to catch up. "Part of what we do when we start to watch certain people's progress is to watch them when they dream. Some people who are moving along that road to evolving travel in their dreams. They go to other worlds and other times.

"We spoke to one of your human writers about this once. He wrote a story called *Childhood's End*. It was about people who were evolving and traveling in their dreams. His name was Arthur Clarke."

Leigh spoke up, "Arnor, Joey has told me about his dreams for the last few years. They have been strange, but not bad, just very intense and filled with strange people and strange places."

Arnor nodded his head.

"Yes. Those are the travel dreams. Joey has been to many other worlds during his dreamtimes. We have been monitoring him. Only a few Earth humans are able to do this. And they don't really understand what it is that's happening to them while they are dreaming."

Joey was stumbling as he was walking along. His mind was in a whirl. He couldn't understand all these connections that seemed to be happening. Leigh reached out and took his hand in hers again. Holding onto him tightly and looking at him, she said, "It's going to be all right now. All of those questions that you were asking about yourself, well, I think that we're going to get some answers now. We're going to be all right. I feel that we are safe with these people."

Bara and Josa were walking along ahead of them and just smiling at Joey's "education."

After walking for about one-half mile, Bara and Josa turned left and entered what looked like a hiking trail leading into the woods. Arnor, Joey, and Leigh followed a moment later. The group walked for an additional one-quarter mile along this path, coming into a clearing in the trees. There sat a large vehicle that looked a little like a large shoebox-shaped motor home, but without wheels, tires, or even axles. Arnor and his crew stood looking at it for a moment with a look of pride on their faces. It was about twelve feet wide, about twelve feet tall, and about forty feet long. It had a wide window/windshield in front. A single door sat fifteen feet down the right side. The flat roof had a series of protuberances, like small rounded bowls sitting upside down. Arnor raised his right-hand wrist up to his mouth. He spoke into that device that looked like a large wristwatch. He spoke three words into the device, and the door opened quietly.

Josa immediately entered the vehicle and turned left toward the front. Bara started a slow walk around the outside, carefully watching the trees and the brush. Arnor spoke to Joey and Leigh, "Please remember, we mean you no harm. You are safe with us. We will take you to places that you have only, perhaps, dreamed about. You will be traveling in good, safe company. Now if you will, please follow me."

He stepped into the door and turned left toward the front of the vessel. Joey and Leigh followed him inside.

Once inside, they were pleased to see that everything was spotlessly clean. They were in a short corridor that ran from the front compartment back to a series of doorways almost to the rear. Arnor beckoned them to follow him into the front compartment. They found a large area almost filled with recliner-type seats and computer-type consoles. The large window in front was a clear, glasslike material. They were watching Bara as he completed his perimeter check. He was using a tubelike small device that he held up to his eyes, like a mini telescope. He walked back to the entry door. As he entered the vessel, the door closed shut and sealed itself with a muffled thunk noise.

Josa was sitting at a console, and his fingers seemed to be flying over the keyboards. They heard a muffled sound of machinery noises coming from the rear of the vessel. Arnor motioned them to sit down in two seats that were in the rear of the compartment. Bara interjected, "If you both could follow me, please. You both need to be decontaminated before we can leave here."

They followed him back to another door that led into a large space with two small cubicles leading off from it. Bara told Leigh to please enter one cubicle and to follow the instructions. She would have to disrobe and to place eye protection over her eyes. The cleaning process would be done with a high-intensity light beam. He told Joey to enter the second cubicle and to follow the same instructions. They were a little uncertain, but they were ready to do what they were asked to do.

After their cleansing process, they were given a uniform like the rest of the crew. Their clothing was placed in containers for special cleaning and would be returned to them later. As they rejoined Bara, he asked them to stand apart while he scanned them with the same tubelike device. He explained that it read heat signals and that if anything was not right about what he was looking at, it would alert him. As he scanned them, he took a deep breath like a hiss.

"Joey, you have some human diseases, quite a few of them. I want you to see me after we get on board our ship. I can make most of them go away."

Joey was stunned. He knew about his diseases, but he had been told that nothing could be done to fix them.

Leigh gasped and said, "Bara, can you heal him from these diseases?"

"Yes."

As he started to scan her, he added, "We can also halt the aging process for you humans. Our healing technologies can do a lot of things that you Earth humans are only just starting to look at."

He finished looking at Leigh and, in an excited voice, said, "You should come and see me also. I can help with some of the things that you are bothered with."

She just looked at him in awe.

Bara continued, "You two can go back to the control room now. The captain would like you there as we return to our ship."

They left his medical compartment and walked to the control room. As they sat down, they were struck with the view. There had been no loud noises of engines, no sense of movement at all, but they were already well out into space and rapidly moving toward a spot near the Earth's moon.

Arnor was at the control station. He was speaking to a control box on the console in front of him, "*Shuttle 4* to *Universal Peace*. *Shuttle 4* to *Universal Peace*. We are approaching from your left rear quadrant. Please open the landing bay doors."

A voice from the speaker grill answered, "*Universal Peace* to *Shuttle 4*. We have you on sensor. The landing bay doors are opening. Welcome back, Captain. Do you have your passengers? Over."

Arnor answered quietly, "Yes, we have them. It was a successful trip."

There was an interrupted noise like cheering that came from the speaker.

Joey and Leigh watched as, suddenly, in the apparent middle of open space, a softly lighted huge square began to fill their view. Nothing else was visible. Joey murmured, "Why can't we see it?"

Josa answered him, "We have had the technology for a long time to create a screen around ourselves so that others seem to see right through us, like a distorted image from a convex mirror."

Arnor guided the shuttle into the landing bay. Joey and Leigh watched as he landed beside three other shuttles, and the huge doors silently closed behind them.

With Josa shutting down the shuttle controls, Arnor stood up, and everyone walked back to the door leading to the outside.

After waiting for a few minutes while the atmosphere outside was made livable, he opened the door and stepped out into the landing bay. They were greeted by a large group of more crew members who all seemed to be humanoid people, and they all were wearing large smiles. When Joey and Leigh followed him, he stood to one side, and with a wide smile on his face, he said, "Joey, Leigh, welcome aboard *Universal Peace*. We have been waiting for you for some time."

CHAPTER THREE

As Joey looked around the shuttle bay, he was stunned by the sheer size of it all. This was a space almost as large as a football field. It was brightly lighted and very clean. Arnor watched him with an amused look on his face. He then began to tell Joey about the ship. Bara and Josa both nodded to their captain. Bara left to check on his hospital and if he had any new patients. Josa left to check on the engineering section, and as he walked past the captain, Arnor spoke to him in passing, "Josa, please make all preparations for getting underway. I want to start for our next visit world. I would like to be moving in an hour."

"Yes, Captain." And he hurried off.

"Joey, my ship and crew are going to be your home for a while. You might want to know a few things about *Universal Peace.* By your Earth measurements, she is about one mile wide, one and one-half miles tall, and her length is about two of your Earth miles."

Joey and Leigh both were standing there gap-mouthed in awe.

Arnor continued, "My crew is made up of members from more than twenty different worlds. They number around three thousand people."

As he was speaking, he motioned for Joey and Leigh to follow him.

"This shuttle deck is the same size as one of your sports fields, one hundred feet by three hundred feet."

He led them through a doorway and into a long corridor. He cautioned them to watch and be careful where they were stepping. The corridors were fitted with moving strips like some airports. As they stepped onto the strip that he pointed out to them, he spoke into a small communications device that he had attached to his wrist, "Captain to the bridge. I am bringing two visitors to you. Please start preparations for getting underway. Our next stop will be in the Sirius Sector."

The answer came quickly, with the sound of cheering in the background. "Yes, Captain. Make preparations for getting underway. Our next stop is in the Sirius Sector."

"Joey, if you two don't mind, your quarters will be in the Special Guest Berthing area. That way, you won't be bothered with shift changes among the crew. I am also going to assign a young officer to escort you both for a while to introduce you to the ship and where everything is onboard. At some point, Dr. Bara would like to see you in his health station."

They had reached an interesting place in the corridor, a door that led into an apparently empty space. Arnor smiled as he told them about "mag-lifts."

"Please trust this technology. All you have to do is to step into the space. There are arrows pointing up or down. If you want to go up, just step into the indicated space, and the mag-lift will carry you upwards at a slow, steady pace. When you reach the level that you want to go to, just step off."

He stepped into the space and slowly rose up out of sight. Joey looked at Leigh, shrugged his shoulders, and stepped into the space. As he rose up out of sight, Leigh stepped into the lift and followed him.

When Joey saw Arnor waiting for him on an upper level, he stepped forward and off the lift; a moment later, Leigh joined them. Arnor said, "This is the control-bridge level. Please follow me."

They walked through a corridor with doors leading off to each side. Leigh noticed that even the colors were a mix of light colors and even some Earth tones, natural reds, yellows, greens, and light browns. The gentle lighting everywhere seemed to be radiating from the walls.

At the end of the corridor, a door slid open silently, with an automatic movement. They all stepped into a very large space. Joey and Leigh were again speechless. The space had one wall that was all that same see-through material. They found themselves looking out onto a deep space scene of stars with vague shadows of color in the far distance. The "seeing wall" measured about one hundred feet long by fifteen feet high. In front of it and facing it were six chairs placed at computer control stations, spaced out about twenty feet apart. Located just behind them and at the center of the wall was a single chair that included a plethora of control knobs and buttons built into the arms, like a remote control freak's dream come true. There were also other control stations located against the other walls.

These usually had large screens attached. Joey did a quick count of people, and he counted twenty all together.

Arnor spoke up, and addressing everyone, he said, "Bridge crew! Let me introduce to you all to our special guests, Joey and Leigh, the people that we came here to find and to bring with us."

The uproar of cheers from everyone was enthusiastic and loud. Joey and Leigh both found themselves blushing with the attention, as they were immediately surrounded by the entire crew. There were many voices saying, "Thank you. Thank you both for joining us."

Arnor suddenly spoke up again, "All right, everyone. That's enough for now. We have other places to go. Let's make all preparations for getting underway."

Everyone suddenly scattered to their respective stations, and the area became very busy. But Joey and Leigh noticed that while everyone was doing their tasks, they all had big smiles on their faces.

Joey heard a slight noise of movement behind him, and turning his head, he saw the door behind them opening. Through the door came a slim, stunningly beautiful young woman with a shaved head. As she walked over to them, they heard Arnor speak up and say, "Joey, Leigh, this is Lieutenant Mara. She is one of the new officers on board, and she will be your guide for the next few time periods, until you both become used to where everything is on board *Universal Peace*."

Mara smiled and introduced herself. She then told them, "Could you please follow me, and I'll show you to your living quarters and to where we all go to eat. Also, Dr. Bara has mentioned that he would like to see you both at some point shortly."

As they stepped through the door back into the corridor, they heard Arnor say, "Joey, Leigh, if you can be back here in two hours, you can watch us as we are underway. It's an experience that you will find interesting."

Mara took them back to the lift area, and they descended three levels. Here they were led along a corridor to a doorway. Mara showed them how to open the doorway and to program it to their handprints. Entering the room, they were pleasantly surprised. Joey had had some experience on Earth ships, and he had been prepared for a compact small one-room-fits-all space. They were shown a twenty-feet-by-thirty-feet room with two other doorways at the rear. Mara told them that the space on the right was their sleeping space. The space on the left was their bathroom. On one wall was a shallow, recessed enclosure with a small tray resting on a shelf. Mara showed them that this was for the computer system that would, if they asked it, provide them with any food or drink that they might want, and if it couldn't, they could see the food officer, explain to her what they wanted, and the computer would be programmed for that item. She went on to explain that if they decided to eat with the rest of the crew members, there were several special eating spaces throughout the ship. These eating spaces were open and active all the time. There were no times when they were not open.

Mara turned to the computer food station and spoke, "Computer."

A slightly mechanical, husky, but pleasant female voice answered, "Yes."

Mara spoke in a normal tone, "Please give me two cups of hot tea. Earl Grey. No sugar or milk."

Instantly, two mugs of hot, steaming tea appeared on the tray.

Mara reached in, and taking each one, she turned and handed them to Joey and Leigh with a smile.

"It's just that easy. Oops. I'm sorry. Do either one of you like milk or sugar?"

Leigh answered with a warm smile, "No. We both like it straight up. Thank you very much."

Mara suddenly reached for her wrist device as it sounded a faint ringtone. "Yes! Yes, Sir, I will." Turning to them both, she said, "Dr. Bara wants to remind you both to come and see him when you can. He seems excited about something. We can go to see him right now, or you can wait until after we get underway."

Joey looked at Leigh. "Let's go and see him. He seems to be really excited about looking at us."

They left their quarters, and Mara led them back to the lifts. Going up for one level, they turned left, away from the front of the ship. A few doors down, Mara spoke to the door. A moment later, it opened into the health-care area of the ship. Dr. Bara greeted them warmly, "I'm so happy to see you both here. Please sit down. I have some things to tell you both."

Joey and Leigh sat down to where he indicated. Mara looked at Dr. Bara. He nodded to her, and she left the area. As she passed through the door, she said, "I'll be back shortly. Dr. Bara, the captain wants them both on the control bridge when we get underway."

"OK, Lieutenant Mara. I'll see that they get there on time."

Turning back to Joey and Leigh, he said in an excited voice, "When I scanned you both, I picked up evidence of diseases in you both. Joey, you have five of them! Leigh, you have one! But, Leigh, I'm more excited because you are pregnant."

Leigh rocked back onto her chair and almost fell over backward. She had had no idea at all about it yet. Her normal menstrual period wasn't due for a few days yet. Dr. Bara was telling her that she was about three weeks pregnant.

Joey knew that he had had a few health problems but nothing that he couldn't get through. Joey was stunned about the news, and he suddenly felt an excitement begin to flow through him about the prospect of becoming a father again.

Dr. Bara told Joey that he was first. "Could you please get up onto an examining table?"

Joey climbed up onto the table and settled down. Dr. Bara began to examine him closely. As he worked, he was humming to himself in happiness. He said, "I can clean up all of your diseases, Joey. Our health technologies are very advanced. I can have you disease-free in about eight weeks."

Joey climbed back off from the table.

Dr. Bara spoke to Leigh, "Oh, Leigh, you have given me a great gift. We never experience human reproduction within our crew. We carefully control it. Your pregnancy will be the first one for me on board this vessel."

Joey and Leigh looked at each other, and a slow smile came to their faces as the realization sank in about their coming parenthood. Dr. Bara moved over to a recess in the wall. Speaking to the computer, he asked for a series of items. They materialized quickly. He then went back to Joey.

"Joey, these will clear up your diseases with no side effects. Take these with water once a day for the next few weeks. Leigh, can you come and sit on the examining table for me?"

Joey sat up and slid down from the table. Leigh sat down on the table. Dr. Bara used his examining tool, the one that looked like a handheld small telescope. He slowly watched its screen as he moved it over her body.

"Leigh, you have a single disease that I can clear up in one dose of medicine. If you want me to, I can give it to you now. As for your pregnancy, it is too early for me to tell you what the gender of the child is. I will be able to tell you in a few weeks. Oh, Leigh, I'm so happy for you both. And this will be a first for this ship."

He went to the computer recess and ordered another medicine. When it arrived, he turned and handed it to Leigh.

"Leigh, if you take this now, there will be no harm to the new life within you. The longer that you wait though increases the risk."

Leigh took the medicine then.

CHAPTER FOUR

The door to the health-care area opened noiselessly, and Lieutenant Mara entered. She looked around quickly and then smiled at what she saw.

"Please, will both of you come with me now? We are getting ready to get underway, and the captain would like you both in the bridge control station when we do."

They stepped through the door back into the corridor and walked back to the lifts that carried them to the control station. Lieutenant Mara was bubbling with happiness. She spoke to Leigh, "Oh, Leigh, the rumors are already being passed throughout the ship about your pregnancy. Everyone is excited about this. You are already becoming the top topic of conversations. Many of us have never known a pregnant woman in our lives, at least not since we have been aboard this ship. You are the first ever on board."

As they passed other crew members, they were greeted warmly with smiles and handshakes. A few of the female crew members smiled at her, reached out, and touched Leigh's stomach, to her embarrassment. Already everyone seemed to be calling her by her first name in friendship.

Entering the bridge control station, they quickly stepped to one side and watched the bustle of activity from a safe vantage point where they weren't in the way. Arnor saw them and gestured to them to come close to his command chair. They stood beside him and said nothing.

A voice came from a speaker in the arm of his chair, "Engineering to control. We are ready to answer all signals."

Arnor responded, "Control to engineering. Stand by."

In a loud voice, he spoke up, "Are we all ready?"

Each station, in turn, responded, "Ready, Captain."

"Bridge control to engineering. All ahead slow."

"Captain to steering. Bring us onto a heading for the Sirius System. Sensors on full. Deflectors on full. We don't want any surprise encounters with any stray asteroids."

Joey and Leigh watched the screen/wall as the star scene slowly began to shift to one side. Joey was interested because there was no sense of pushing motion or any noise at all. But the scene outside the ship steadied, and they slowly began to move toward the distant stars.

"Control to engineering. Increase speed to one-third."

"Engineering. Increase speed to one-third."

Again, there was no sense of thrust or pushing. But the scene on the wall began to move past them slightly faster.

Arnor watched their faces and said, "Our propulsion system is magneto/gravitic. We are able to harness the power of the magnetic fields that move through space. We don't burn fuel to travel. This is clean, and it has no residue. It's also unlimited. We are able to focus our gravity and our antigravity shields, and we are able to make them push us or pull us in the direction that we want to go. Josa can tell you much more about this when you are interested."

A very slim tall man walked toward them from one of the side-screen stations. They noticed that he was humanoid but that his skin had a greenish tinge and that his voice was slightly hoarse. Arnor introduced him as Mr. Savak, the first officer. He said, "Joey, Leigh, I am so glad to meet you both. The captain has told me so much about you." Turning slightly to Arnor and breaking out into a big smile, he continued, "Captain, we are on our way to the Sirius Sector. Our present course will take us to the first planet out from the secondary sun there. It will be good for some of us to be back near to our home worlds. And it will be good to be moving away from this Earth world. Many of us have sad memories from this world."

Arnor looked around quickly at the crew and said, "Yes. But we can talk to Joey and Leigh about *Celestial Explorer* and what happened with her later? Right now, we have an eighty-three-day journey to our destination ahead of us. Let's focus on that for now."

Savak responded, "Yes, Sir, Captain."

"Mr. Savak, you have command. I will be giving Joey and Leigh a slow tour of *Universal Peace*. And then we'll be getting some dinner on the Deck 6 eating area. Their cook is really good."

"Yes, Sir, Captain. We are at underway routine. Deflector shields are up. Sensors are on full." He looked at a screen near his arm and said somewhat judicially, "We are coming up to speed. Our estimated time of arrival is eighty-two days, six hours, and forty-one minutes, ship's time."

With Arnor leading the way, Joey and Leigh, followed by Lieutenant Mara, stepped through the door leading out from the control station. Arnor began a chatter description of what they were seeing. They all headed toward the lift area again. After going down many levels in the lifts, they exited the lifts, and Arnor spoke into his wrist communications device, "Captain to engineering. I am headed to your engine control room with our two visitors."

Standing on the moving passageway strips, Arnor began to tell them about the features of his ship. His pride in the ship was evident. He explained about the three full-size deck areas that were used for farming and the two decks areas that were used for water and air recycling. One deck was all trees, a pond, and walking paths. As he talked, Joey and Leigh were in awe. Concepts like living on a ship like this for years and even decades at a time were all new to them, having areas where the crew could walk on soil surrounded by trees, small animals, birds, flowering shrubs, wading pools, all of which was created to give them a chance to enjoy a natural world environment even while in deep space.

Arnor told them that these areas were always busy. The farming areas were used to provide air/water recycling and to provide a place for waste recycling. At the same time, these areas provided fresh food for the crew. These areas were very extensive and had artificial lighting that simulated sunlight. They included fish farms and large hydroponic gardens. Joey and Leigh began to get a sense of why the ship was so large. This ship was like a moving home world to this crew.

Arnor explained that the selection process to become a crew member on these ships was very intensive. Potential crew members would work for years to go through the selection process. He mentioned that there were other ships like *Universal Peace*. They had been in use for many thousands of years. They roamed the known galaxy, always seeking, always exploring, always working to help the peoples of worlds to evolve. He mentioned that he himself had been in command of *Universal Peace* for what amounted to twenty thousand Earth years.

Again, Joey and Leigh had a sudden sense of some great sadness when he mentioned the experience of an age-old Earth area. Something had happened here, and it caused a deep sadness to those who remembered it.

As they moved closer to the engineering section, the corridors merged and became twenty feet wide and then thirty feet wide. The ceilings became much higher. They saw a multitude of strange-looking equipment that was being used. They were all electric powered, silent running, with no exhaust. The people operating them all stopped for a moment and greeted them with smiles and well wishes.

They came to the end of a large corridor and stepped through a doorway on the right side. They found themselves in a very large control room with what looked like walls of multiple view screens. The room was a similar size to the bridge control room. Joey recognized it as an engineering control station, but there the similarity ended. He had been in ships' engineering control rooms on ships at sea. On them, there had been the background noise levels: that assortment of mechanical noises, engines, pumps, propellers, switches, and the ever-present work of repairs by workmen trying to keep it all operating. Here it was so quiet. Even the conversations were in a slightly mumbled tone. Joey was reminded of pictures that he had seen of the control stations for the space rockets at Cape Canaveral in Florida.

This control room was quiet. The only noises were from the conversations of the staff who were working there. There were around sixteen people working at the control systems and another six who were moving around on various errands. They all were connected with headphones to many others who were working in the machinery spaces.

One of the figures turned, smiled broadly, and walked toward them briskly. As Josa reached them, he held out his hand to them and said, "Joey, Leigh, welcome to my office. This is the engineering department. I am so happy to see you here." He then turned and motioned to another figure at the far end of the space. "Jaco, please come here and meet our visitors from the world known as Earth.

"Joey, Leigh, this is Jaco, my third assistant engineering officer."

As the figure turned toward them, Joey and Leigh instantly felt an almost palpable wave of hatred coming at them from the other man. He was a stockily built man and seemed to be struggling to contain his anger toward them. Josa sensed this also and spoke to the man, "Jaco, that was thousands of years ago, and you cannot hold these people responsible for what happened. Do you understand me?"

The man Jaco stopped a few feet away from them and would not come any closer. He did not greet them. He scowled and almost growled at them. Joey and Leigh had never felt such anger from anyone else that they had met in this entire crew. Josa abruptly spoke to Jaco, "Go back to your duties. We *will* talk about this later.

"Joey, Leigh, I'm sorry about this. His anger comes from—"

Arnor spoke up quickly, "Josa, we can explain this later when we all can sit down together, and we can tell them the whole tragic story."

"But he is my officer, Captain."

"No, Josa. He is *our* officer, and *we* will deal with this."

"Yes, Captain."

Joey turned to Leigh and, with a deep look, said, "I don't know what this is all about, but I feel that we are safe here."

Arnor spoke up again and said, "Josa, Lieutenant Mara, why don't we all head toward the dining hall on Deck 6? We can get something to eat there and chat for a while. Lieutenant, could you please lead the way?"

"Yes, Captain. Could you follow me, please?"

They all left the engineering control station and walked back toward one of the lift points. There was a subdued sadness coming from the ship's engineering crew now. Joey still felt no danger toward Leigh or to himself.

CHAPTER FIVE

Exiting the lift, Joey and Leigh, following Lieutenant Mara and being followed by Captain Arnor and Engineer Officer Josa, found themselves on Deck 6. Joey was awestruck. He turned to Leigh and saw that she too was stunned. They saw an area of farming fields that stretched outward for hundreds of yards in all directions. There were small pieces of farm equipment being operated by people moving up and down rows of crops with green tops. Joey thought to himself that it all looked like huge truck garden farms that he had seen in his years in Southern Maine. The lighting was mimicking sunlight and was constant throughout the entire area. Watering seemed to be from soaker-type hoses running between the rows of plants. Joey walked over to the nearest soil, and reaching down, he picked up a handful and brought it up to his nose. Taking in a deep smell of it, he was pleased to find that it smelled just like the soil samples that he remembered from his childhood, that rich, moist, earthy smell of growing things. Looking at Leigh, he just nodded his head and grinned.

Arnor, Josa, and Lieutenant Mara were watching all this and smiling. Lieutenant Mara looked at the captain, and getting his silent approval, she started to walk down a designated dirt path through the fields toward a distant set of buildings. Joey and Leigh followed her. After walking for almost one-half mile, they reached the buildings and entered the largest one. Joey and Leigh were once again surprised. They found themselves in a very large dining hall that was open to the surrounding air and was occupied by roughly 150 people. Many of them saw the captain, waved to him, and spoke up in greetings.

Arnor now led them toward a section of the room that was marked off as Officers Only. When everyone was seated at a table, a crewman working as a waiter came to them with printed menus. Joey and Leigh were again surprised when they opened these up and found five pages of food selections.

Arnor said, "Well, we do like to eat well on this ship. And there are three other farming decks. Each one has its eating area and its special types of foods."

They all ordered hot herbal teas and made their food selections. After the waiter left, there was a period of silence among them. Arnor watched Joey and Leigh looking around, just taking it all in. He was enjoying their reaction to it all.

Josa spoke up and told them, "Joey, Leigh, we are very proud of *Universal Peace*. She is our home. Most of us worked very hard to become accepted as a crew member. Then once we get here, we tend to stay here for the rest of our lives. This is our home now and our family. You should know that *Universal Peace* has many sister ships. There are more than fifty, all told. Our culture has been building them for more than one hundred thousand of your Earth years. We have become very good at this. Those of us who work on these ships tend to be from the same families. We all have many family members who are on our sister ships: fathers, mothers, siblings, children. We try to make sure that family members are not working on the same ship. But sometimes, we do serve together. There are the dangers that we sometimes encounter. Our ships have become so self-contained that they are really self-contained, moving worlds. These are constantly traveling from star system to star system. We are helping out other peoples to evolve and to become partners in our culture. Hundreds of worlds have done this. Our culture has become a universal, peaceful combination of many hundreds of equal worlds."

Arnor spoke up, "This is why we have been watching your Earth world for a while, Joey. At one time, your world was evolving to the point where we had made your people aware of us, and we were going to let you join us and then—"

One of the waiters suddenly hurried over and spoke to Captain Arnor, "Captain, Captain Arnor, there has been a call from the control bridge. You are needed there immediately."

Arnor stood up quickly, reached for his wrist communicator, looked at it, and with a slightly embarrassed murmur, said, "Oops. I apologize. I forgot that I had put it on silent while we were sitting down to eat. Please excuse me while I attend to this problem."

He spoke into his wrist communicator, "Captain to the bridge. I'm on my way to you now." He hurried off toward the doorway.

Joey smiled slightly, remembering having done the same thing often. He glanced around the table and saw that Lieutenant Mara's eyes were full of tears. Turning back to look at Josa, he said, "Would someone please tell us what this is all about? Some people are angry with us, or they cry when they meet us. What the hell is going on? What happened to cause these reactions to us?"

Josa quietly said, "I am an engineer. But maybe this is all meant to be to become a healing process for us all." After a moment that seemed to be chiseled out of some dark, sad stone monument. He began to speak again in a low voice that radiated a deep sadness, "Joey, Leigh, you are from a world known as Earth. Some 12,800 of your Earth years ago, we were there talking to your human ancestors. We had been teaching them our way for some time. They had evolved to the point where we were going to allow them to become part of our culture. We had given them many tools to advance their civilization: astronomy, mathematics, sciences, agriculture, healing systems, energy systems, and our deep spirituality. They were progressing very well. Then the accident happened, and it all came to a tragic, even catastrophic, sudden, forced ending."

Leigh looked at Lieutenant Mara and saw her tears flowing down her cheeks.

"That day on *Universal Peace*, we were slowing down as we came into the Earth's sun's system. We were nearing the Earth's moon. We were there to join with one of our sister ships, *Celestial Explorer*. She was parked in orbit over the Earth. Some of her crew members were on the planet working with various different cultures that were there in place at that time.

"We knew about a scheduled meteor shower that was coming, so we didn't have any concerns. That meteor shower has been named by you Earth people as Perseid. It's a regular occurrence for your world. So we weren't concerned. As we neared your planet, we were talking with *Celestial Explorer*. We were talking to relatives and friends, planning on gathering together to chat and eat. There was much laughter. Then, suddenly, mixed into and hidden behind the small meteorites of the shower, we saw a very large meteor headed toward Earth. It measured some miles across in diameter. As it passed near to the planet Mars, Mars's gravity well pulled at that meteor, and its course altered slightly. Suddenly, it was not going to be a near miss. It was headed straight toward Earth, and *Celestial Explorer* was right in its path."

Lieutenant Mara's head was bent down, and she was sobbing. The waiters were also standing nearby, and they had tears flowing down their faces.

"We heard the sounds of the frantic activity coming from the *Explorer*. They tried to get their propulsion started to get out of the way. We listened to the screams as they realized that they could not move out of its way in time. The laughter that we had just been a part of suddenly had changed to something just the opposite. Now all that we could hear were screams of fear and anguish. And these were coming from friends and family members. The meteor hit her hard and destroyed her entire left side. The impact drove both she and the meteor into the Earth. The impact of two objects, both of them miles in diameter, was tremendous. We saw the whole planet shake in convulsions. The meteor hit the planet near the equator. *Celestial Explorer* hit just below the northern top of the planet at the same moment. We saw the planet literally shaking in reaction, as if it were going to tear itself apart. There were volcanoes suddenly erupting all over the planet at the same time. Watching this happen, we felt that there could be no survivors left alive on the planet. We saw what looked like the planet's crustal plates shift to one side by a massive amount. We quickly pulled away in our stunned state. We made the decision to leave. We didn't want to be caught up in what might become the possible, explosive destruction of the entire planet."

Joey and Leigh had both read the stories and theories over the years and talked to each other, some of the theories that had been written about something major happening to the Earth at about that time period, something that had triggered the last Ice Age and killed off most of the planet's inhabitants. But this version had never even been considered.

After taking a moment to compose himself, Josa continued speaking, "In our stunned emotional state, we vowed to never return to this place again. Most of us have made some effort at healing from this, but there are some who are still angry about 'those damned Earth humans.'

"Try to imagine the reaction that we had when, about 2,500 of your years ago, one of our ships passed near here and detected large civilizations here again. We very carefully started to watch and to study your world again. We were stunned when we began learning, following that ancient accident, when there was such a catastrophic loss of life there, that there had been pockets of survivors. Our surprise was even more so when we learned that there had been survivors from *Celestial Explorer* who had been scattered across your world. These survivors had stayed with those pockets of human survivors. We learned that they had continued to teach and to guide them, even encouraging them to watch the skies for help. Eventually, they had died from the effects of Earth's climate. But their teachings remained a foundation for and became an array of your world's spiritual beliefs.

"We continued to watch your world. We began to identify some special Earth humans who showed great promise. We were able to quietly meet with them and to give them some special teachings that encouraged them to try to start the process of bringing the Earth humans back to that point where they would start to evolve again: a man named Buddha; another, a woman named Mary; and her son, Jesus. And there have been others since then. They did so well that we expanded our efforts. There have been many others since them. And now we have come to you two."

Joey and Leigh were just sitting there with openmouthed awe at what they were hearing. Finally, Joey blurted out, "But, Josa, where do we fit into this? We aren't anything special. I'm just another tired old grunt workingman. We don't come close to being some sort of spiritual leader. Why have you chosen us to come with you?"

CHAPTER SIX

Bara settled back in his seat and, with an enigmatic smile, said to Joey, "You will have to wait for Captain Arnor to tell you all of that. I may have already said too much."

Leigh looked around herself and saw that those crew members that had been standing near them and listening to the conversation all had stopped the sadness and had a kind of happy, pleased look on their faces. There seemed to be a polite pause while they waited to see what Joey and Leigh's reaction might be to what had just been said.

Lieutenant Mara glanced at her wrist communicator, and then standing up, she quietly said, "Joey, Leigh, this has been a very eventful day for you both. It's getting late now. Perhaps you should be . . . Well, let me lead you back to your quarters. I think that you both need some rest. Tomorrow will be a busy day as well for you both. There's a lot to learn here."

The minute that she said it, Joey realized that he was, in fact, exhausted. Looking at Leigh, he saw the same thing with her.

"Yeah. Thank you. Let's go."

They walked to a nearby door, and Lieutenant Mara led them to a lift location. Going upward for a few decks, they emerged onto a corridor that Joey thought looked a little familiar. They quickly reached the rooms that had been set aside for them. Lieutenant Mara asked, "Are you both all right now? Do you need any help with the room controls? Lighting? Waste? Something to eat or drink?"

Leigh said, "Thank you, but I think that we'll be OK. We just need some rest now. What time do you want to see us tomorrow?"

Lieutenant Mara answered, "You can rest as long as you need to. Just tell the room computer when to wake you and when to call me."

Leigh reached out her hand up to the door control panel, and it opened quietly. Lieutenant Mara smiled and walked away. Leigh entered, with Joey right behind her. After the door closed, she turned to Joey, and they both reached out and hugged each other tightly. Joey murmured in her ear, "It's going to be all right. We're safe here. I don't feel any threat at all. I am starting to trust these people. I love you, kid."

Leigh, leaning backward a little bit, looked slightly upward into his eyes and nodded her head in assent.

"Oh, I feel the same way that you do, my love. There's a lot for us to get used to right now. But we're going to be OK."

Pulling back away from him, she let go of his arms and mumbled, "But I have to use the bathroom *right* now."

Joey went to the sleeping area. He quickly saw that it looked comfortable and that the bed looked soft. Taking a deep breath, he spoke to the room itself, "Room computer, please reduce the lighting for sleep mode! Turn down the heating to about sixty-six degrees Fahrenheit. Please give us two cups of chamomile tea, hot with no cream or sugar."

Instantly, the lighting in the rooms lowered down. Two cups of hot tea appeared in the computer wall station. Joey quickly caught the aroma of the chamomile.

A few moments later, Leigh came out of the bathroom.

Joey said, "My turn now." And he walked into it.

When he had figured out the controls and finished his business, he came out and found that Leigh was already undressed and put herself on the bed. He thought to himself, *Well, so much for needing some tea for sleep.* He became pleasantly surprised when, after getting out of his clothing and sliding into the bed, Leigh turned to him, and snuggling into his body shape, she kissed him and began to caress him. She gently moved her hand down across his chest, down across his abdomen, and still a little lower. He responded with a deep moan. He found himself responding quickly to her hands on his body. Turning to her and leaning back slightly, he looked at her and said, "Will this be OK for you? I mean, will you be . . . ?"

With a quiet smile and a slightly husky voice, she said, "It's OK. You can't hurt me. And what are you afraid of? I'm already pregnant, so let's just enjoy this."

She rolled her body over onto him and began to softly moan and to move her body against his.

Time seemed to stand still as their focus turned toward each other, and everything else just drifted away.

Later, as their bodies and minds relaxed, they drifted off to a deep, restful sleep.

Joey's mind began to slowly move upward away from his dreams and into that place where we go just before awakening. He sensed things around himself, but he was still remembering his last dream. As he opened his eyes, he had a shock. The room was strange and did not look at all like his bedroom at home. There was some sort of gentle music playing in the background. He scrambled quickly to get out of bed, and in doing so, he tangled his feet in the bedcovers. There was a sound of triple muffled thuds as, first, his shoulders then his hips and, finally, his knees hit the floor. He gave out with a mumbled "Shit." Next, he heard laughter coming from the doorway. It was Leigh, standing there fully dressed, holding a cup of steaming coffee, and chuckling at his awkward position.

"Good morning, sleepyhead."

"What the . . . ? What's going on? Where are we? Oh, wait a minute. I remember now."

"I woke up early and figured out some of the things here in this room. The computer even plays music for you if you ask it to. This coffee is hazelnut flavor. By the way, the shower is not water. It's a bright white light that really cleans you. And it leaves you dry. No damp towels to have to hang up afterwards."

"What time is it?"

She just smiled and said, "About 8:00 a.m."

He mumbled, "I need to get cleaned up."

He turned and headed for the bathroom. Once there, he ended up spending some time figuring out what things were for what and, in some instances, what they were not for. No bathroom sink. So he had to read labels on containers to figure out that now shaving was done with a slightly applied cream that even had some sort of pleasant odor mixed into it. After that, he worked on the controls for the light shower. There was a normal style of commode.

Sometime later, he emerged looking and feeling much better, and she handed him a fresh cup of coffee. Leigh spoke up to the room, "Room computer, please notify Lieutenant Mara that we are ready for some breakfast and whatever this day will bring to us."

Ten minutes later, there was a soft chime from the door. They opened it, and Lieutenant Mara smiled at seeing their faces.

"Please follow me. We are going to the eating area on Deck 7. They have a great breakfast cook."

After moving along to another lift station (there seemed to be one every few hundred yards along the corridors), after lowering down a couple of decks, they moved toward what seemed like a very busy eating area. There were dozens of people moving toward a cafeteria, picking up some trays, and choosing some food that looked very good. They followed Lieutenant Mara to a table that looked out over a scene of green grass, trees, and paths wandering around pools of water. It was a tranquil scene that could be in any place on Earth. But a surprise that it was here on this starship traveling though space between worlds. Many people smiled and waved at them. Many seemed to know their names and spoke up, saying, "Hi, Joey. Hi, Leigh." Joey and Leigh were embarrassed by being considered celebrities. Lieutenant Mara was just smiling with them.

As they ate their meal, Lieutenant Mara told them that their next stop was back on the bridge. There, Captain Arnor wanted to talk to them about their stay on board *Universal Peace*.

Finishing their meal, they left the eating area and moved back through the corridors and lift system toward the bridge. Arriving there, they entered and saw the full bridge crew working. The star scenes were moving past the view screen at a steady, slow pace.

Arnor, glancing over his shoulder at them, said, "We are at two-thirds speed now, headed back toward our home world's systems, the twin stars of the Sirius System. We should be there in about eighty-one days, ship's time. Good morning to you both. I hope that you rested well.

"Joey, Leigh, I have been thinking about a way to keep you two from becoming bored and to let you both experience life here on board *Universal Peace*. I would like you two to become members of this crew. Joey, is there some part of the ship's operations that you might be interested in learning? And, Leigh, is there something that you might be interested in working at while you are here?"

Leigh spoke up first, "Captain Arnor, on Earth, we don't have any knowledge at all that comes close to matching what everyone here has. How can we be of any help?"

"Leigh, you two might be surprised at what your intuition and instincts might lead you to be able to help with here. As for knowing about our tools and our culture, that will come with time. You two might even be able to teach us a few things."

Leigh spoke again, "Captain, I have always been working in health care. Is it possible for me to work with Dr. Bara at his health-care station here on board?"

Joey and Arnor both glanced at Bara to see his reaction to this request. He suddenly broke out with a large smile. "Captain, I would be honored to have Leigh working with me. She can learn, and she can teach me a few things. As a bonus, we can watch the progress of her pregnancy. Oh, Captain, please grant her, her request."

"Done. Leigh, you may now consider yourself as a member of the medical team on board *Universal Peace*. Joey, do you have a special area that you would like to work in?"

Joey had a huge grin on his face as he spoke up, "Captain, would it be possible for me to work in engineering? I used to work in ship's engine rooms on Earth. I still enjoy that atmosphere."

Arnor smiled. "Joey, you are now assigned to engineering. You will be working directly for Josa."

Everyone was looking at one another and smiling. Dr. Bara motioned to Leigh and said, "Why don't you follow me to the health-care station, Leigh? We can get started on this mutual learning process."

Lieutenant Mara looked at Joey. "Can you find your way to engineering? Or would you like me to show you?"

Joey answered, "I don't know the way around here yet."

They both left the bridge, with Lieutenant Mara leading the way.

CHAPTER SEVEN

When Joey arrived at the engineering control room, Josa met him at the door with a large smile on his face. "Oh, Joey, I'm so happy that you will be here in my crew while you're here on *Universal Peace*. Welcome. Captain Arnor called me as you were coming here and told me about your decision. Thank you for choosing us.

"Joey. Here is my lead supervisor, Harri. He will be your direct supervisor and your teacher. Harri, this is Joey, from Earth. He will be working on your crew. Teach him well."

They shook hands. Harri took Joey to a large cabinet in one corner of the control room. Opening it up, he withdrew some clothing and some objects. Handing these all to Joey, he explained, "These are the work uniforms for our engineering department, and here is a wrist communicator, your safety badge, and your recorder. Carry these with you at all times."

He showed Joey how to operate the communicator and how the safety badge worked. They then went out into the engineering spaces, and Harri showed Joey how to use the recorder while taking machinery readings from the different machines. Joey was again in awe of how quiet everything was here. There were none of the machinery noises that he had expected. Harri introduced him to other crew members. Everyone seemed to be so happy that he was working with them.

Harri stopped and said, "Joey, it's time for our lunch break. Let's go back and get something to eat."

Joey was surprised. He looked at his wrist device and saw that more than four hours had passed, and he hadn't even been conscious of it. Making their way back to the engineering control station, they entered and walked to another room off from it. Here they found a full lunchroom setup. Sitting down, meeting everyone, and chatting, suddenly, Joey heard his wrist device sound a quiet tone. Joey jumped a little. Everyone chuckled. Harri showed him how to answer the communications call that had just come to him.

He looked at the screen and saw Leigh looking at him. They started to talk. Leigh was telling him about her day at the health station and what she was learning from Dr. Bara.

"Joey, this is so wonderful. I am learning so much, and we are already seeing patients. I think that some people are coming in here just to see me. I don't think that they are really sick at all. How was your day?"

"Hey, Leigh. Wow. I'll tell you more later, but this place is great. I already knew that their technology is so far ahead of ours. But I didn't dream that it was like this. They use less than 10 percent of the energy that we use to move from one place to another. And it's all clean energy. No leftovers. No pollution. No waste. No environmental damage. And it looks like it's all renewable and infinite. This magneto/gravitic stuff is really something that we could use back home."

Harri was watching all this conversation and just smiling. Another crewman entered the room, and suddenly, the very air seemed to tense up and to turn hot with anger. Jaco scowled at Joey and started to walk toward him in a threatening manner. Joey didn't notice. He was still talking to Leigh. Harri and two other crew members stood up and blocked his way. Jaco was almost spiting with anger. Harri quietly said, "That was a long time ago, and he wasn't part of any of it. Leave now and put this all behind you, Jaco. *Now.*"

Joey stopped talking to Leigh and noticed what was going on. He stood up, but Harri and the other crewmen stayed in between them, facing Jaco. Jaco, radiating an almost visibly pulsating anger, stalked away and out of the room. Harri and the other crewmen looked at one another and nodded their heads. This type of behavior was very unusual for anyone on board. It would have to be reported to the captain.

Joey was still a little puzzled and did not understand what was going on. Harri and the others turned back and sat down in their chairs. Harri spoke to Joey, "Don't worry, Joey. This will be taken care of. We will not allow him to harm either one of you."

Joey blurted out, "What is he mad about? Did I do something wrong to him? If I did, please, let me make it right!"

Harri responded with a partial comment, "Joey, he is angry over what happened on *Celestial Explorer.* Both of his parents were on board. *We* will take care of this situation. Don't worry."

Joey's mind was in a whirl. His thoughts were *What the heck was going on anyway? What had all of that to do with me and Leigh?*

"Don't worry, Joey. We will take care of this. You are a welcome member of this crew now, and we will make sure that this is dealt with."

Harri quietly changed the subject by saying, "Joey, I am going to start teaching you about our energy systems. I would like you to read these books about our systems. Be careful with these. You will have questions about them, and we expect that. Any questions that you have, please ask one of us. We have been told to teach you this information."

Joey looked at the books and opened the first one and started to read it. Harri and the other engineers just looked at one another and exchanged glances. A decision was made to report the incident to the captain as soon as possible.

Leigh was listening to Dr. Bara. She was amazed at the differences in health care in this ship. She had studied about holistic-care practices, and she was somewhat familiar with the concepts of it. She had been leaning toward it for some time now. She had taken classes in Reiki healing. But here, it was in full usage. All the health care in these cultures was based on holistic modalities, that pulling in of that universal energy to help people heal. Dr. Bara was teaching her that, with this ship and this size of a crew, there were frequent small accidents and even illnesses similar to flus and colds. Here there were no drugs, no magic pills to cure everything (and to leave multiple side effects). Here the normal treatments were focused on the whole person, that combination of body, mind, spirit, and not just on the physical cause of the problem. Dr. Bara explained (and Leigh told him that he was preaching to the choir). She then had to spend the next ten minutes telling him what that comment meant. He told her that every being was comprised of three parts: the physical body, the mind, and the spirit. Their culture believed in the foundation with their health-care systems, that the only complete healing came with treating the whole being, all three parts.

Dr. Bara was very happy with her. Because she had already been drawn to these healing modalities, she had some of the basic understanding already. He had already decided that she was a great candidate to be his next assistant and that he was going to start that type of training with her right away.

Suddenly, the door to the health-care station burst open, and the ship's emergency rescue crew crowded inside, carrying an injured crewman. The man had been working on one of the farming decks. His piece of farm equipment had turned suddenly, and the man was thrown off. As he hit the ground, the piece of equipment had rolled over his right leg. It was badly broken with an open fracture just below the knee.

Dr. Bara grabbed Leigh and pulled her with him. "Come on. I need your help with this one. This is going to take both of us. Grab those scissors in that drawer. Get his pants cut off. We need to see all of his injuries."

Leigh was already moving quickly without even seeming to have to think about what needed to be done next. As she was cutting the trousers from the injured man, Dr. Bara was pulling down a helmetlike device from the ceiling. He quickly fitted it over the top of the man's head and turned on a switch. The man instantly began to slip into a relaxed state of being. Leigh had the trousers all cut off as Dr. Bara brought over a rolling tray that contained sterile bandages and cleaning solutions. He and Leigh began to clean the injured area. She pointed to the site where the broken bones were penetrating the skin. Dr. Bara nodded his head and scowled a little in concentration as he stared at the injury. Leigh didn't even seem to mind that the blood oozing out around the bone slivers was a light-green color and that the bones were a darker green. For her, this was an injured person.

Dr. Bara was attaching a device that would pull the leg to a straightened position. Leigh finished up cleaning the site and turned to Bara, waiting for instructions. He pointed toward another cabinet and said, "Once this leg is straightened out, I'll start an IV line. I know where the veins are with his species. You can open up that walk-in cabinet over there. We'll have to leave him on this table and to put him into the cabinet. Once inside there, the focused beams of the healing energy will have him feeling much better in a few hours."

After they were done, they both realized how tired they were. They just sat down in chairs and took a few deep breaths. Leigh looked at Dr. Bara questioningly. He smiled and said, "You are great. If you will accept the work, I would be very pleased to have you as my new assistant. For right now though, I think that we need to go find us a couple of cups of hot tea. That crewman will be fine. The holistic treatments that he is receiving now will have him healed in a few days. He will have a few weeks of rehab and light duty. But he should be back to full work in about four weeks. These things happen around here on a regular basis."

Leigh leaned back in her chair and sighed. "Dr. Bara. Thank you for this lesson and for the offer to work with you. I have always wanted to work at helping people to heal. I accept your offer. I would love to learn from you."

Bara replied with a sigh of relief, "Thank you for accepting my offer. I sense that a great good will come from this. Now let's head to the Deck 7 farming area. They have some great herbal teas at their eating area."

They walked out into the corridor and headed for the lift station.

Once at the eating station, they picked up their teacups. Bara motioned for Leigh to walk with him out onto the graded pathway system. They both kept up a quiet conversation about Leigh's background in holistic studies. He led her to a large pool of water, with trees and some benches to sit on. Leigh was amazed at the thought that had gone into adding something like this to a starship, the intent of the designers to create a place of rest for the crew members. Bara was so happy with listening to her intuitive comments. He was feeling that his initial sense about her capabilities as a healer was validated. She was going to be a great help to him.

CHAPTER EIGHT

Leigh and Joey had become accepted as new crew members. Everyone seemed to be busy all the time. Joey was in his engineering classroom, and Leigh was quickly becoming a valued help in the health-care station. Their meals were always at one of the crew meal stations, where they were always joined by other crew members who were eager to learn about them and about Earth. The passing days became a blur.

One evening, as they were getting ready for bed, Joey was asking her how she was feeling. Suddenly, Leigh looked at him with an openmouthed look of surprise on her face. "Joey, do you know what today is?"

"Yep. Do you?"

"We have been on board for one month today."

"Yep. We've become so busy learning stuff and helping out that we kind of lost track of the time. Harri and I were talking about it today. We're almost halfway to their home worlds."

They settled into their bed and told the room's computer to dim the lights and to start the soft music that they had come to love. Joey was thinking that they had adjusted to fit into the crew routine very well. They were learning so much about the cultures of the crew members. It was so easy to accept everyone. They were all so full of joy and what felt like a universal love between themselves and everything around themselves. From what he had heard and what Leigh was learning also, the cultures of these worlds that they were headed toward were all like that. These worlds had once been like Earth, but they had overcome the hatred, anger, greed, and violence. They had become awakened and aware. They had become peoples who now worked toward love, peace, and working together to help other worlds to that same goal. As Joey drifted off to sleep, he thought that this place was a really nice place to be.

Waking up was still the same: groggy, stumbling around a little, smelling that welcome aroma of hot coffee, opening his eyes, and seeing Leigh moving around and getting dressed. His thoughts were *God! Oh, Leigh, how I love you so much.* He noticed that her lower stomach was just showing a slight swelling. He was reminded that she was pregnant. He thought, *I'm so glad that we are here with Dr. Bara for this.*

There was a chime sound from the room communications system. Leigh spoke to it, "Yes, what can we do for you?"

The pleasant female voice from the computer said, "Leigh, if Joey is there, Captain Arnor would like to have breakfast with you both at 0730 hours, if you can make it. Can you both meet him at the meal area on Deck 6?"

Leigh turned to Joey and nodded her head yes. Joey nodded in return. Leigh said, "Computer, please tell Captain Arnor that we would be very happy to join him for breakfast."

Turning to look at Joey, she said, "Come on, dear. No time to waste this morning. If we move right along, we can be there a few minutes early."

As they entered the Deck 6 meal area, they saw a small group of people that included the captain. Walking over to the table, they were motioned to seats across from Captain Arnor. He smiled at them and said, "Joey, Leigh, I apologize for not seeing you two more over the last few weeks. Things have been very busy on board. We have also been in touch with some of the other ships of our worlds. They are excited to know that we have two people from Earth with us now. But please, let's eat first."

After everyone had ordered their meals, they started to chat among themselves. Arnor turned to Joey and said, "Joey, about the crewman who is giving you a problem, I have spoken to him, and he has assured me that he will not bother you anymore."

Leigh looked at Joey with a questioning glance that said "What's going on?"

Joey quickly said, "It's OK, dear. I wasn't worried, and I didn't want to bother you either."

Everyone started to eat their meals. Arnor continued speaking to them, "Joey, Leigh, I am so happy to hear about your working with the crew. Everyone is telling me how good you two are at what you're doing. Leigh, Dr. Bara is excited about your becoming his new assistant, and his reports tell me that you are learning our health-care methods very quickly. Tell me, please. And be truthful. Have you been studying our methods for years before we picked you up on your world? You seem to know so much already."

Leigh blushed at his compliment. "Captain, I am just grateful to have a fine teacher with Dr. Bara."

Arnor turned to Joey. "Joey, Josa and Harri are telling me that you seem to have a natural knack for our engineering systems. Their reports are highly supportive of your work. I may even be tempted to offer you a permanent position here on *Universal Peace*."

Now it was Joey's turn to blush and to stammer. "Aw, Captain, I just like doing this stuff. And Harri and Josa are great teachers."

"Well, keep up the good work, both of you. What you two are doing now was not part of our original intention for you two. This work that you're doing with us is a great thing. It's like an extra gift to us here. Our reports to our Worlds Administration about you two are being received with a lot of excitement. Our cultures had no idea that Earth's people had the capacity to learn our technology so swiftly. What you two are doing here is changing our thoughts about how we can or cannot help your world. We are starting to reconsider that maybe Earth is worth trying to save, even though it is its own worst enemy right now. You two are showing us that Earth people are worth saving, that they can learn quickly, and that they can learn peaceful ways to live with others. Some of our sister ships and some members of our Combined Worlds Administration are all sailing to our home world in the hopes of meeting you two when we arrive there. You two may find yourselves being treated as ambassadors when we arrive."

Joey and Leigh just sat back in their chairs in stunned silence. They had had no idea at all that they were being talked about this way. They had both been so busy with learning and with helping out the crew.

CHAPTER NINE

It had now been eight weeks on board for them. Joey and Leigh were very involved with their work on board now. They were just a few weeks from seeing the home worlds of the ship's crews. The excitement was being felt already. Everyone seemed to have a smile of anticipation on their faces. Leigh thought that it was starting to feel like that special time of the year on Earth, when everyone is getting ready for Christmas. There was a tangible excitement in the air.

Leigh was doing great. The news about her child was something to get used to. Having a new baby was giving him a lot to think about. They were both so excited about all this. Wow. Having a child with Leigh was a lot to think about. His daughter from his first marriage had broken off all contact with him years ago. And his relationship with his stepson was strained at best.

He was also watching Leigh. She seemed to have acquired that, oh so special, glow that seemed to emanate from her body, that special thing that happens to women when they are pregnant. He thought that she was even more beautiful now. It was hard to believe that she was one-third of the way through her pregnancy already. Dr. Bara was so excited about having her on board.

Dinner last evening with Captain Arnor, Mr. Savak (he had such a dry, subtle sense of humor, but he was a really nice guy), and Lieutenant Mara. They had all had a great time. That sudden request from Arnor was stunning. But Josa didn't seem to have any problem with it, even when it would mean having him spend part of each week working on the ship's control bridge.

Joey had thought to himself, "Boy, there's never a dull moment around here."

He finished changing into his work clothes and headed into the ship's propulsion space to check on the main engines. He spoke to Harri, telling him where he was headed and what he was headed to do. Harri, while talking on his communicator, just waved his hand and nodded OK.

Joey was humming to himself as he worked his way along a catwalk over the two-hundred-foot-long spinning shaft portion of the equipment. Joey was looking down toward the engines; they were about thirty feet below him, and they stretched out for many feet on the other side of where he was standing. He was watching and listening for anything unusual. He was using one of the ship's special tools to sense anything out of place or any unusual noise from the machinery. Joey was focusing intently on what he was seeing and hearing from the machinery that he didn't hear anything until his intuition sensed something near him and behind him. As he started to turn toward it, he saw a blurred shadow rushing toward him. He felt the blow from something heavy hitting him on his neck and shoulder. Then as he started to lose consciousness, he felt himself being lifted up and over the guardrail. He felt himself falling. His sight was fading into darkness. His last thought was that he thought he saw Jaco's face with a maniacal grin above him. Then the darkness.

Leigh suddenly felt a sense of wrenching fear. She couldn't place a reason why. She was starting to shrug it off, when her wrist communicator, along with Dr. Bara's, started to sound an alarm. They both knew that this meant an accident somewhere. The results of it were coming to them at the health-care station. The room's computer voice suddenly started to tell them, "Emergency! Emergency! There has been an accident. The rescue crew is coming to them from the engineering area with a badly injured man."

Leigh's intuition started to get stronger. She was trying to get ready for the emergency and to try to control her growing fear. *What the hell is causing this?* she thought to herself.

The door burst open with the rescue crewmen team hurrying in. A figure was on the floating stretcher, crumpled on its side, covered with a blanket. There were spots of red blood everywhere. The faces of the rescue crew were ashen with concern and fear.

Leigh and Dr. Bara hurried to the stretcher. Two of the rescue crew moved to intercept her from seeing the stretcher. She started to protest when her intuition started to scream in her ears.

"No!" she screamed.

Dr. Bara reached for her to pull her back from the sight of Joey's badly injured body.

She stared. Shaking off his hands, she almost growled at him, "Dr. Bara, let me help. I know his body better than anyone here does."

Bara looked intently at her for just a moment, and then making his decision, he nodded to the rescue crewmen. "Let her in to help. She is one of the best assistants that I have ever had. I think that she'll be all right with this."

She pushed her way in, and they started to work on Joey. There was a jumbled babble of voices from the rescue crew. They told them that something very terrible had happened on board. This had not been an accident. It was an attempt by a crewman to kill another crewman. Everyone was stunned at the idea that it could happen there on board *Universal Peace*. There were three crewmen who had seen it happen, so there was no doubt about what had happened. The crewman who had done it was seen and identified. It was a man named Jaco. He was loose and hiding somewhere on board the ship.

Bara and Leigh were barely conscious of the conversation. Their focus was on the injured Joey. Dr. Bara turned to them and interrupted them, "EXACTLY WHAT HAPPENED HERE? Does anyone know what happened here? Someone please tell me exactly what happened to this man!" he yelled.

The confused babble stopped. A momentary silence followed. One crewman standing to one side spoke up in a calm, quiet voice, "Dr. Bara, my name is Harri. I work with Joey in engineering. I was on my way to talk to him. I saw what happened. Jaco hit him on the shoulder and neck with a large wrench and threw him over the guardrail toward the main engine shafts. As Joey was falling over the guardrail, his body hit a support beam for the catwalk and bounced to one side. He missed the spinning shafts completely. His injuries are from the blow from the wrench and from the fall to the floor below. He fell about thirty feet, and he was bouncing off from different pieces of metal framework as he fell. When we reached him, he was lying on his left side near the shafts. But he didn't hit them as he was falling."

Dr. Bara looked at him in silence as he pictured this man with the quiet calm in this emergency situation. He nodded his head in thanks and muttered, "Thank you. Now I have an idea of where to look for his injuries."

Turning to Leigh, he said, "OK. Now we know what to start looking for here. Are you OK with working on this problem with me?"

She too had calmed down while listening to that crewman's quiet voice. "Yes, Doctor. Let's get started here. I'll get the clothes cut off. Do you want the IV equipment? How about the energy hood? I happen to know where the blood vessels are on Earth humans.

It looks like we have multiple bone fractures here: left arm, right shoulder, right leg above the knee. Well, come on, Dr. Bara. Let's get started on this injured man, or do you want to wait until after I leave?"

Bara looked at her for a moment and gave a slight smile. This was someone who didn't get rattled in a bad emergency situation. He stepped in, and they started working.

Leigh reached for the scissors to start cutting off the remnants of the uniform. She thought to herself, *Joey is going to be all right.*

Dr. Bara was getting ready to use the special tools that he used to straighten out the broken bones. He passed one of his scanning devices over Joey's body. The readout would give him a precise diagnosis of the injuries.

The door to the health-care station suddenly burst open, and an excited crewman hollered into everyone standing there, "They caught him! They caught him! He was trying to hide out on one of the farming decks. They caught him!"

Everyone seemed to relax. They all had unconsciously been stiffened up with tension, thinking that a possible killer was loose on board.

Dr. Bara and Leigh were very busy working on Joey's injuries. They had located and straightened out the broken bones. He also had a skull fracture and some internal injuries from the fall to the floor. Dr. Bara looked at Leigh intently and said, "We have to get him into the healing chamber now. We have done all that we can do for now."

She nodded her head. They moved him on the floating stretcher into the large box-shaped room, making sure that the stretcher was supported well. They closed the doors, and Dr. Bara turned on the controls to focus the healing energy into the chamber.

The door to the station burst open again, and Captain Arnor hurried in. Looking at the crew first, he saw that they were relaxed. Now knowing that the situation was improving, he walked over to Leigh and Dr. Bara. Looking at Dr. Bara, his face asked the question first. Dr. Bara smiled a tired smile. "He's going to be all right, Captain. He has some injuries, some broken bones. But he's going to be all right."

Arnor now looked at Leigh. He had such a look of relief on his face. He gently and being a little unsure of himself, like he was trying something new for the first time. He stepped up to her and reached out his arms around her. She knew what he wanted and stepped forward. They hugged. He murmured in her ear, "It's going to be all right. He's going to be all right, Leigh. Don't worry. He's going to be all right."

She just nodded her head.

Arnor stepped back a little, and turning to everyone, he said in a voice that sounded like the voice of doom, "Jaco is alive and unharmed. He knows what the fate is on board our ships for people who behave like he has. He knows what is coming for him."

Arnor turned, and moving like an unstoppable force of nature, he headed back toward the bridge control station.

Joey was inside the healing energy chamber. Dr. Bara's prognosis was that he would be OK. The injuries would be repaired within a few weeks.

"There is really nothing more that we can do right now, Leigh. Please, why don't you try to get some rest?"

Leigh walked back to their quarters, but she couldn't sit still. She ended up going to one of the walking path areas. Sitting on a bench overlooking one of the ponds, she allowed herself to cry. She knew that this was a vital part of the healing process that she needed. Other crew members who walked past her would stop, touch her shoulder, and murmur a word of support of what she was going through. Within her heart, she felt a deep feeling that everything was going to be OK. It was almost like a deep, rumbling voice that was speaking to her, telling her that "It's OK. It's OK."

Leigh gave an inward shrug of strength. She stood up. Turning, she staunchly walked back to the corridor and the lift station.

A short time later, Leigh was at the health-care station working with Dr. Bara. He suggested that she have him examine her for her pregnancy. She agreed, and following his directions, she disrobed and lay down on an examining table. Dr. Bara passed a small scanning tool that he had over her body, paying special attention to her abdomen.

He said, "Well, now we know what gender your child is."

He turned away and told her that she could get dressed. Leigh was holding her breath in anticipation. He didn't say anything, but he had a small smile on his face. Leigh finished dressing and stood there waiting. Finally, after a few more minutes of increasing anticipation, she blurted out, "Are you going to tell me or not, Dr. Bara?"

He turned, and with a large grin on his face, he said, "I was just going to see how long it would take you to say something. Ha ha!

"Oh, Leigh! Oh, Leigh! Your child is a girl-child. I'm so happy for all of you."

Leigh stepped forward toward Dr. Bara. Much to her surprise, he stepped backward a little. He seemed to be unsure of what she wanted to do. Now it was her turn to have that humorous small smile.

She said, "I owe you this. Please don't worry. It's nice. It feels good, and it doesn't hurt you."

With that said, she stepped a little closer to him. Reaching out, she gathered him into her arms and hugged him. The look of caution on his face changed to a look of awe and then to a smile. As she released him and stepped back, she almost burst out into laughter at that first puzzled and then quickly changing to pleased look on his face.

He said, "What was that? Is that something that Earth people do? What does it mean? It felt so nice."

Leigh realized that hugs were something that was not known to his culture. She went on to explain, "We do this all the time to those people that we consider friends. This is a sign of love between people. It is used as a symbol and a display of good feeling between two people or even small groups of friends."

"No, we have never seen this done before. This is something that comes from your world? But it is so beautiful a gesture. Wait until I tell the others about this. Will they be surprised. I'll have you show this to the others. It feels so good. What was it that you called this? An ugg?"

Smiling, she spelled it out and said, "No. An h-u-g!"

Just at that moment, both of their wrist communicators sounded a loud chime. Looking at his, he said, "Oops. We have an emergency coming in. It looks like an accident from one of the outside-the-ship repair teams. These can be bad. Let's go! We have to get ready. The rescue team is bringing the victim here now."

They both hurried to get ready.

CHAPTER TEN

Joey's consciousness was starting to awaken. He felt so much at peace. His memories of recent events hadn't started to return yet. His mouth was a little dry, but that wasn't so bad. He started to try to move, and he found that he couldn't feel his body much. That was strange. He tried to speak but only could mumble something. Suddenly, he sensed a hand picking his head up, holding it up a little, and some cool fluid being slowly poured into his mouth. He managed to swallow it and immediately felt better. But he was puzzled. What the hell was going on? He tried to move again. He felt like he was moving in slow motion. He then heard a soft woman's voice speaking to him.

"Hi, Joey. This is Leigh. You have been injured, and you're in recovery at the health-care station. Take it slow and easy now. Move your left arm first."

Joey listened. He recognized Leigh's voice. He struggled to slowly open his eyes. It felt like they were caked shut with something, but they did finally open. As his eyes slowly focused, he looked around the room. He was surprised. The room was crowded with people. Captain Arnor was there. As was Josa, Harri, Dr. Bara, and all the crew from engineering that he had been working with. He felt that he was lying down on some sort of a very soft, slightly floating bed. His body had some points of aches, but nothing really bad. He saw that Leigh was crying now with tears of happiness. Now some of his memories started filter back into his consciousness. He tried to move again.

Dr. Bara quickly spoke up, "Wait, Joey. Wait. Give your body a chance to slowly return to normal sensation. You have had some broken bones. They need a chance to finish healing. Your right arm and shoulder took the most damage."

Joey swallowed again and said, "What time is it? What happened? Have I been unconscious long?"

Leigh whispered to him, "You've been unconscious for just over a week now."

"What? I don't . . . A week? I've been unconscious for a week? What happened?"

Dr. Bara quietly spoke, "Yes. Joey, you were hurt badly in an accident."

Arnor spoke to him, "Joey, crewman Jaco tried to kill you. He has been caught and is now in our custody. When we reach our home world next week, we will deal with his actions. But we can talk about all of this later. You need to finish your recovery now. We are all so happy that you are going to be all right. You had us worried for a while, but Dr. Bara and your Leigh have done outstanding work in treating you.

"OK, everyone. He is going to be all right. Now. Let's all get back to work now and get us home."

They all filed out of the room. Joey was looking at Leigh. "I'm sorry, kid. I didn't want to worry you."

She was crying again. "You just rest now and get better. And don't you worry about me."

Bara touched her on the shoulder. She stood up, and they left the room. Joey drifted off into sleep again.

When Joey woke up again, he saw that he was in a different room. It was like his living quarters. He looked over at a figure sitting on a chair next to his bed. It was Leigh, and her head was hunched forward. She was sound asleep. Joey just smiled. He loved her so much.

He tried to move his arms and found a pleasant surprise. He was weak, but he had very little discomfort. He moved again and slowly sat up in bed. Again, he had some aches, but little or no pain.

Abruptly, Leigh jerked upright in her chair. Seeing him awake and trying to sit upright, she started to stand up, but Joey spoke up and said, "Sit down, please. I feel all right. Please. Sit down. Just let me try this. If I can't, then I'll set back down again."

Leigh relaxed back into her chair a little. But she kept herself ready to reach out to help him, if he needed it. The worried look on her face slowly began to relax.

"How do you feel, hon?"

Joey was quiet as he started to remember what had happened. "Like I lost a bad fight. How long have I been laid up?"

"Almost three weeks."

"Three weeks? What's going on? Am I going to be all right? Or am I going to have to stay here for a long time?"

"Easy. You're almost completely healed. The bones are back to normal. We are letting the treatments finish up their work now. You should be up and about within a couple of days. This health-care system that they have is unbelievable. They can do things here that we don't even begin to know about on Earth. You had four serious broken bones, and they were all back to normal within two weeks. The internal injuries took a little longer, but they're all healed now. The thing that they are doing with this universal healing energy stuff is just—well, it's almost magic, but I know that it's everyday normal for them."

Joey listened to her speaking, and suddenly, he turned sideways. Swinging his legs over the side of the bed, he carefully stood up while holding onto the stand beside the bed.

Leigh jumped up and stepped toward him, reaching for his shoulders to steady him. "*Don't do that.* If you fall over again, you could hurt yourself again."

Joey had a stubborn look on his face that she knew well. He was a little shaky on his feet, and he felt weak. But he was still standing on his own.

Leigh murmured, "How do you feel right now?"

"Hungry!"

She smiled and spoke to the room computer, "Computer, please give us a bowl of hot vegetable soup, with a green salad, and two cups of hot herbal tea. Also give us two butterscotch ice cream sundaes, with whipped cream and nuts."

Joey looked at her in surprise. He slowly moved sideways to the nearby table, holding onto the furniture as he went. Reaching the chair, he sat down with a quiet sigh. Leigh sat opposite him. The computer did its thing, and the meal appeared on the table in front of Joey. He picked up a spoon and began to eat the soup. Leigh was watching him closely for any signs of weakness. Joey smiled and ate his soup. After he finished the salad, the two of them ate their ice cream sundaes.

Leigh gave a huge inward sigh of relief. He was going to be OK. Joey was going to make it. That tough Irishman mixed with that damned stubborn Scot was going to be all right now. She could relax her worries.

The room door sounded a chime. Leigh said, "Door open."

In walked Dr. Bara. He stopped in his tracks and stared at Joey.

Imagine

"What are you doing? You're not supposed to be out of bed yet. You need to stay in bed for a few more days. You could hurt yourself."

Leigh just smiled. "Dr. Bara, welcome to an example of Earth stubbornness. This is a trait that many of us Earth humans have. And this particular Earth *man* has a large dose of it. He'll be all right. I will keep a close watch on him. Trust me on that."

Later, after Joey had a chance to get cleaned up and dressed, they all were called to the bridge control station. Captain Arnor wanted to see them.

CHAPTER ELEVEN

As Joey, Leigh, and Dr. Bara entered the bridge control room, they witnessed a scene of intense work. The bridge crew were all at their stations guiding the ship into their home-world system. The view outside from the window wall showed two separate suns. They were slowly passing by one of them and moving toward the second one. They had already passed some worlds and were moving toward a planet that was near the second sun. This planet was one of seven that surrounded that sun. The ship's sensor systems also showed eight other ships like *Universal Peace* moving toward the same area.

Joey was reminded of those times when he, as a child, had watched as huge oil tankers moved around the harbors in his home port city in New England, these ponderous, slow-moving, seemingly gentle large, massive giants moving slowly as they performed their pirouettes and waltzes around one another, always dancing but never ever touching.

The communications station members had a constant chatter going on with them. With all that sense of intense work, there was no sense of anxiety or stress. Everyone was focused and at ease.

Mr. Savak (Joey was starting to think of him as a Spock look-alike) saw them at the door and hurried over to them. Touching Joey on his arm, he said, "Come with me, Joey. I have a chair for you over here near the captain."

Lieutenant Mara came to Leigh, and looking into her eyes intently, she reached out and put her arms around Leigh in a hug. They both were close to tears. She then led Leigh over to a chair beside where Joey was just settling into his.

Mr. Savak spoke to the captain in a low tone, "Captain, they have arrived, Sir."

Captain Arnor turned his head, looking at them all, and said, "Hi, Joey. Hi, Leigh. I'm a little busy right now. Mr. Savak can explain what is going on. Joey, I am so happy to see you up and about. Please forgive me for not coming to you. Things get a little crowded for us when we're coming home. And it's a little worse right now. Usually, the other ships are not all here at the same time. Everyone is here for the conference that has been called to discuss your world, Earth."

Joey and Leigh were taken aback. What conference? What was being talked about involving Earth? This was the first that they had heard about any of this.

Mr. Savak seemed to sense their troubled thoughts. He murmured to them, "Please, both of you, don't worry. There is no danger. These representatives of our Combined Worlds Administration have been called in together to meet you both. There is much interest in hearing you speak. Their interest is in Earth and what our Combined Worlds culture can do to help Earth to evolve."

Joey and Leigh looked at each other. This was unexpected, to say the least. They didn't consider themselves to be representatives of Earth. They were just regular working people.

Joey spoke to Leigh in a whisper, "Boy, I don't know what I expected, but it sure wasn't this. I think that these folks are expecting more from us than we can give them. Neither one of us is a politician or anything."

Leigh very quietly said, "Joey, I'm a little scared about this."

"Yeah. Me too."

Listening to Arnor command his ship was a lesson in quiet competence. He never raised his voice. He never had to. The crew showed how well they knew their work. Some commands never had to be spoken. They all worked together as if they were a part of the same body. Joey noticed that the background noise level on the bridge control station was more like that of the study hall in his local library than that on a massive ship moving through space. It was the finest example of professional competence that he had ever seen.

Captain Arnor finally spoke those anticipated words, "All engines stop! All engines back one-half! All engines stop! Engineering? We are finished with main engines. Captain to all hands, we are home again. Secure the ship. Liberty for all hands will begin tomorrow on our usual schedule. Thank you, all hands."

A moment later, Joey and Leigh were surprised and slightly embarrassed to find themselves surrounded by the entire bridge crew. They were all so happy to see that Joey was all right. There were even some attempts at hugs for them both.

Captain Arnor, speaking for everyone, said, "Boy, it's good to be home again—and this time, with our very special guests. Joey, Leigh, would you both like to join me for dinner at the meal area on Deck 6 after I get cleaned up a bit? The bridge crew and I are going to be together there for our traditional home-again dinner. And I can fill you both in on what to expect over the next few weeks here. Our Combined Worlds Administration is very anxious to meet you both."

Joey quickly responded, "Captain Arnor, we don't know what is expected of us. We are no one special. We're just average people."

Arnor replied, "Joey, Leigh, please listen to me carefully. You both are very special people. You just don't know it yet. We have been watching you two for a very long time now. You two have come to represent what we hope Earth peoples will start to evolve toward. But enough! We can talk about this later. Let me just say again that you two are very special people."

Everyone around them were smiling and nodding their heads in agreement with Captain Arnor. Mr. Savak smiled broadly and said, "Joey! We will explain much of what is happening later when we can talk. For now, let us get cleaned up and have our dinner. We will tell you what to expect while we are doing that. You two are being welcomed as the representatives from your Earth world. There is a great deal of hope for the future. And some of it is based on what we have seen of you two and how you behave toward others."

By this time, everyone was at the lift station and separating to go to their individual quarters. Joey was starting to get tired, but he was looking forward to the dinner. They both wanted to find out just what was going on.

A few hours later, after Joey had had a chance to rest for a bit, they dressed and left to go to the dinner on the Deck 6 eating area.

As they arrived at the Deck 6 meal area, they walked in and saw a large crowd of crewmen. Lieutenant Mara met them at the doorway. "Come with me, please."

They followed her to a large set of tables. Captain Arnor and the rest of the bridge crew were there. A chorus of "Welcomes." Greeted them. They were seated, and the dinner party began. Joey and Leigh both noticed something very interesting. Even with the very festive atmosphere going on, they saw no signs of alcohol or anything like it. Everyone was thoroughly enjoying themselves with much laughter and jokes, but there was no sign of any intoxicants in any form. Joey thought to himself, *Boy, this is a clean culture, and that cleanliness is so refreshing to witness. These people know how to work hard and to play afterwards without the destruction of booze or drugs. I could grow to like being a part of this world.*

Much later, after the meal was eaten and everyone had talked, played a little, and joked a lot, he and Leigh found themselves within a group of about fifteen people: Arnor, Dr. Bara, Mr. Savak, Josa, even Lieutenant Mara. They were all just sitting together off in one corner of the area. Arnor turned to Joey. After slowly looking around to make sure that what he said would not be overheard by too many people, he nodded his head to the others, who all answered his nod with theirs.

"Well, Joey, Leigh, you two have been a part of some interesting things since you've been with us here on *Universal Peace.*

"First things first. Joey, Leigh, you were assaulted by one of my crewmen. Here in our culture, we focus our efforts on peace and nonviolence. Our whole Worlds Administration is focused on that. We have been doing this for what you would think of as more than fifty thousand of your Earth years. So when Jaco attacked you, he stepped over a powerful line. We draw that line when it comes to *any* violent behavior. His reward for what he did was to immediately be confined in a cylinder chair. This chair was filled with fluid to the top. He is allowed to breathe and to stay alive, but he cannot hear or see or move. Now that we are home, he will be released to live out his life on our world. But he has violated his world citizenship. So he has lost all rights and privileges that come with that. On our world, in our culture, we have those who are citizens and those who are not. Those people who are not citizens cannot be hired into any job of responsibility. They cannot obtain help from the administration. They cannot receive social assistance of any kind. There is a system to get this changed for themselves. They can work to earn it back. But if they choose not to, they spend the rest of their lives in poverty, doing menial labor.

"For those people who work to become citizens, this becomes one of their rewards: by living their lives honestly and truthfully, by practicing peace, by helping others. These citizens work to guarantee that they will be comfortable for their entire lives. Many of them become involved with our starships. They work very hard, and they make a lifetime commitment to our efforts. We allow no one to violate these efforts and to walk away without some sort of punishment.

"Jaco knew this. He did what he did to you, and he is now going to reap his reward for doing that. There have been a few others who followed the path that he has. They have all been sentenced to poverty. This is our way of dealing with these people."

Joey was very tense and almost in tears. He quietly spoke to Arnor, "Captain, thank you for explaining this to me. May I say something to you about how I feel about what happened?"

Arnor looked at him and nodded his head.

"Captain, I know that what he did was wrong, but I don't like to see him punished like this. Captain Arnor, I'm asking you to let him go free. I think that maybe if I talk to him, I can help him get over his hurt from what happened to his parents. Maybe if I talk to him, I can get him to change himself for the better."

Everyone in the small group of listeners just stared at Joey. Leigh was smiling at him. She knew what he was like, and she agreed with him. The others were in awe of what he had just said. This was something that they had not even considered. Arnor was shaking his head from side to side with a surprised look on his face. Finally, he looked straight at Joey and said, "Joey, Leigh, for as long as I have studied you Earth people and for as much as I thought that I understood you all, you two are surprising me again. This is going to take some careful consideration by myself and those people that I answer to. I will tell you two that I will have to relay your request to the Combined Worlds Administration. They will make the final decision about Jaco. But I will give them your recommendation.

"Mr. Savak?"

CHAPTER TWELVE

Joey and Leigh had finished getting cleaned up, and with the help of Lieutenant Mara, they had changed into a formal style of ship's uniform. They were all a little nervous. The door chime sounded. Joey spoke to it, "Computer, door open."

When the door opened, in walked Mr. Savak. Quickly looking at them all, he smiled and said, "Joey, Leigh, you both look very good. I sense that you all are very nervous. Please don't be. You have nothing to worry about. These visitors are here to meet and to speak with you. They are not here to judge you in any way. Joey, you two have a saying on your world, 'The definition of an *expert* is the stranger from out of town with a briefcase in his hand.' You two are the experts that these people have come to see. Unfortunately, I don't have a briefcase for either one of you. He smiled and added, "I also am not exactly sure what a briefcase is."

Joey and Leigh visibly relaxed a little. Mr. Savak had surprised them again with his slightly dry sense of humor.

Mr. Savak then got a serious look on his face. "Joey, are you all right with attending this meeting? You are still fresh out of your recovery from the accident. You look tired."

Joey smiled and said, "Mr. Savak, I will be all right. Thank you, Sir. If I get too tired, we can still bow out of the meeting and return here."

Leigh smiled and added in, "Oh, Mr. Savak, he can be very stubborn. But so can I. If I see him getting too tired, he'll come back here either walking beside me or in front of my hands, as I'm pushing him along."

Everyone laughed and walked out of the door, headed toward the Deck 6 meal area and this fateful meeting with the ship's visitors.

Arriving at the meeting, they were greeted with smiles and welcomes. They saw Captain Arnor standing with a group of people whom they hadn't seen before. Making their way to where he was, was a slow process. Many people stopped them to say hello and to wish them well. It seemed that everyone had been told about Joey's early recovery. They all wanted to meet him and to see for themselves how he was doing. Finally arriving to where Captain Arnor was standing, they saw a mixed group of about thirty people. They were pleased to see that there were about an equal number of women in the group. Arnor welcomed them and immediately began introductions. Joey and Leigh noticed that the group were all officers from six ships, like *Universal Peace*. And they were pleasantly surprised when of the six captains, five of them were women.

Joey hurriedly spoke to Arnor, "Captain Arnor, Sir, I know that this meeting is important to you. But can you do me a great service, Sir? Before you make your final decision about Jaco, will you permit me to talk with him face to face?"

Arnor leaned back a little with a surprised look on his face. "What do you want to say to him, Joey?"

"Sir, if you don't mind, Sir, that's very personal, Sir. But I would appreciate your giving me a chance to speak with him first."

Everyone there was now intently listening in. Leigh had a small smile on her face. She knew what Joey was going to do. Captain Arnor had already made arraignments to have Jaco awakened from his confinement capsule and removed from his ship, but it hadn't been done just yet. Arnor, looking deeply into Joey's eyes, said, "OK, Joey, you can speak to him. But you will have to do it now. He is going to be removed from the ship in an hour from now."

Arnor turned to his guests and said, "Please excuse us for a few minutes. I will return shortly. Thank you all for waiting. Please enjoy yourself while you are waiting. Come on, Joey. Let's go. I'll take you to where he is being held. Mr. Savak, Dr. Bara, Josa, please come with us."

A few minutes later, they were on a lower deck level that held some equipment that Joey and Leigh hadn't seen before. Turning into one room, Arnor led them through it, down a short corridor, and into a second door. Inside was a strange capsule device that included a chair inside it. Sitting on the chair was Jaco. He was just coming out of a deep, sedated state. Joey pulled up another chair, placed it directly in front of Jaco, and just sat in the chair. He watched Jaco's face. Jaco's clothing was dripping some sort of fluid onto the floor. He was conscious of what was taking place. Joey watched as a stream of scattered emotions flowed across his face: first anger, quickly followed by worry, then sadness. Finally, he looked so sorry, and he had tears forming in his eyes. Joey was reading all this and gently nodding his head. Everyone except Leigh was astonished by what came from Joey next.

"Jaco, please listen to me. I am so sorry about your family and what happened to your parents. It was a horrible accident and a terrible way to die. Please accept my condolences for your loss. I feel a great sadness for your loss."

Joey reached out and touched Jaco's shoulder. The instant that his hand touched Jaco, it triggered Jaco's tears. His eyes filled up, and the tears began to flow down his face. He began to sob.

Joey stood up, stepped forward, and hugged him in his arms.

"I know what it's like to lose a family member. You lost them both at the same time. I am so sorry for you. I understand."

Arnor, Savak, and Josa were just astounded with what they were witnessing.

Sitting back down on his chair, Joey continued, "Jaco, there is nothing that we can do to change what happened. Jaco, if you can forgive me for coming here from Earth, I can forgive you for what happened between us. Jaco, I forgive you for what happened. Can you forgive me?"

Jaco looked at Joey and then at Leigh. With the tears flowing freely down his cheeks, he stood up and looked at Joey. Joey stood up, and they embraced each other as new friends. Jaco murmured, "Joey, I am so sorry for what I did. Thank you, my friend, for this and for helping me."

Arnor, Josa, and even Mr. Savak were all wiping their eyes.

Then Joey did something that would become part of the legend that would be spoken of, throughout the ship's crews around the galaxy, about this meeting. Turning to the captain, he quietly said, "Captain Arnor, I am asking you to release Jaco right now. Captain, I'm asking you to please keep him with this crew on this ship. I believe that Jaco will become one of your best crew members. Captain, can you please do this for me? He is a good man who just made a mistake. He is a good man, Captain."

Arnor looked at Joey in almost-stunned surprise. "Joey, I have never, in my lifetime, ever heard of or seen what I've seen here just now. In all my studies of your Earth culture, I never thought that I would see what I have just seen here. Joey, you have just taught us a strong lesson in love for other peoples. I think that you Earth people may just be able to teach us a few things. Bara, Josa, and Savak are right. You Earth people have a lot to offer us. I am coming to believe that we can learn much from each other. I am now grateful for having brought you two aboard my ship."

He turned to the others with him. Joey thought that the very air between them vibrated with the mental energy that passed between them as he watched. Then Arnor nodded his head at the others. They, in turn, nodded their heads in return. He turned back to Joey and Jaco.

In his stern I-am-this-ship's-captain voice, he spoke with a deep rumble in his voice, "Crewman Jaco."

Jaco quickly straightened upright and stood at attention.

"Crewman Jaco, I am ordering you to return to your quarters and clean yourself up. You have been away from your duties for too long. Josa, put this crewman back on the crew list. He is officially back on duty on *Universal Peace.*

"Crewman Jaco?"

Jaco was so stiffly at attention that he was almost quivering.

Captain Arnor reached out his hand and took Jaco's hand in his with a handshake.

"Welcome home, crewman Jaco. Welcome back home."

Captain Arnor then spoke to everyone, "All right, everyone. We have a visiting delegation of ships' officers patiently waiting for us to return to them. Let's try to remember who we are. *We are Universal Peace.* Now let's get back to our duties. Josa, you now have a full engineering complement again. All right, everyone. What are we waiting for? Let's get back to Deck 6 and to our guests."

CHAPTER THIRTEEN

It had been another three days now. Joey was feeling much better. He had been walking and exercising. His meals had helped him start regaining some of his lost weight. He and Leigh were taking some time to rest. Arnor had scheduled for them to travel down to the planet's surface. They were going to meet with some of the Combined Worlds Administration. Arnor was hoping that they could have the time to join him in meeting some of the crew's family members. Arnor's family was excited about maybe getting a chance to meet these Earth people.

Today was the big day. They had been tossing and turning all night long in their excitement about going to the surface. The door chime sounded. Joey said, "Computer, open the door."

In walked Mr. Savak, Josa, and Dr. Bara. Broad smiles were the norm.

Savak spoke to them, "Are you two ready for this?"

"Oh yes."

"Well then, let's go down to visit *our* home world."

They walked out of their quarters and headed to the lift station.

When they reached the landing bay, they met Captain Arnor. Everyone then went to one of the shuttles and boarded it. This shuttle was the same one that they had been in before. Joey and Leigh were remembering their first ride in it when they came up to *Universal Peace* from Earth. They were also starting to think about when they would ever return to Earth. Would they ever return to Earth? Did they really want to return to Earth?

After getting settled into their assigned seats, Captain Arnor and Mr. Savak sat down in the command seats.

"Shuttle to *Universal Peace*. Open the landing bay doors. We are getting underway now."

The huge doors opened slowly, and they were underway, headed to a new world for Joey and Leigh to see.

Arnor gave them a slow circle of this world. Their views showed them a planet that had about an even distribution of land and water. It was a world that was similar in size to Earth. It was slightly closer to its sun than Earth was, so it was a little warmer. With that said, both poles were covered in snow and ice. It had a strong, clear, clean atmosphere.

The shuttle then angled downward and began moving down toward a major city. Arnor mentioned with a note of excitement in his voice, "Joey, this is my home world. Depending on what we are told here, I would like to take you both on some visits to three other worlds in our Combined Worlds culture. I think that you two would really like a visit to Mr. Savak's home world. You might find that it is a very interesting place."

They landed softly like how a helicopter might land, hovering over a landing spot and slowly dropping down.

"We're here," Arnor quietly said.

They all stood up, and Arnor went to the doorway. Looking back at Joey and Leigh, he smiled and said, "Don't worry. Just remember. They are expecting some type of major dignitaries. If you two just remain yourselves as you normally are, you will have them fawning at your feet."

Then chuckling quietly, he opened the door.

When Joey and Leigh stepped into the door opening, they were greeted with the sight of a crowd of around three hundred beings, but of so many different types. Joey and Leigh spent the first few moments seemingly spinning their heads back and forth like children at a fun park, just trying to see everything. Later, they would "compare notes" and agree that seeing twenty or thirty different kinds of beings all standing together and cheering for their arrival was a truly once-in-a-lifetime experience. They saw beings that were all vaguely humanoid in their appearance: two arms, two legs, and one head, all standing upright, but from there, it varied widely. Some were very, very thin, almost skeletal, but seven or eight feet tall, and with a green skin, with no body hair. They saw some that were very muscular and heavyset but covered completely with thick body hair, with faces like a grizzly bear. They saw some that were definitely from a reptile-based culture but standing upright like humans. They saw others who were human shaped, but with bluish skin. There were others who were human shaped but were only four feet tall, with a large head and very large dark eyes, and so many others. All were standing side by side and cheering for them as they stepped down onto the soil of this (for them) new world. Joey and Leigh would later tell each other that the strongest feeling that they remembered from this initial moment was one of a powerful peace and love among everyone there.

They saw that the sky was a deep-blue color. The sun was a lightly reddish color. There was a gentle breeze blowing. Very surprisingly, there were no signs of air pollution. The many vehicles that they saw moving around were giving off no noise or signs of exhaust. Later, he would be told by Arnor and Josa that everything here was powered by the same mechanical systems as *Universal Peace*—the magneto/gravitic propulsion machines: no pollution, no residue, no waste.

As they started to walk toward the waiting group of people, Arnor stepped forward between them and touched both of their arms. He said, "Joey, Leigh, I would like to introduce you both to the leader of our Combined Worlds Administration, Chairman Omana. Please, Sir, I would like to have you meet Joey and Leigh from the far world, Earth."

The soft-spoken, gentle-eyed being with a quiet smile stepped up to them and spoke, "Welcome to our culture, both of you. We all have been anticipating your arrival. Captain Arnor has told us much about you both. We are looking forward to chatting with you."

Joey was reminded a little bit of Mr. Savak. This man was from the same world as Savak was—tall, thin, with slightly green skin, and that oh so deep sense of internal peace. When he spoke to them, his voice was a soft, slightly bass sound. Joey and Leigh both started to speak, and then Joey let Leigh finish.

"Hello, Chairman Omana. Thank you for having us here. Your home is beautiful. And everyone seems to be so nice."

Omana touched both of their arms, and turning with them, they faced the crowd. He gestured to them, and everyone in the crowd began cheering. Joey and Leigh were blushing with embarrassment. Omana just smiled.

"Would you both please come with me? We can go to our reception building. You can rest, and then later, we will host you at a dinner. Tomorrow, we can meet and talk. There is much that we have to discuss. Your coming here has forced us to rethink our plans for dealing with your world, Earth."

Joey and Leigh immediately sensed an underlying current of tension when Omana said this. There was something here that didn't feel quite right. They started to go on guard. Arnor saw this and stepped up beside them. Speaking very quietly to them, he said,

"Please, please, both of you, don't worry. Everything is going to be all right."

They were guided toward a open-topped large flying vehicle. It reminded them of a convertible limousine. They stepped into it and sat down. The driver slowly brought it up to a few feet above the surface and began moving it away from the landing area, heading toward a large compound of buildings in the distance. Again, Joey and Leigh were astonished by the quiet. There was no engine noise from the vehicle at all, and it moved so smoothly.

They had the chance to see much of this world. At a first glance, it looked like any other large city on Earth, except that this one was so clean. Everyone seemed to be busy, and they saw so many examples of people just helping one another. The sense was that everywhere that they looked, they saw a place of peace. They saw many examples of different kinds of sun-powered energy and heating systems. There was so much green growth: grasses, trees, and flowering shrubs. The very air was almost crisp with cleanliness. Arnor watched them looking at everything, and he smiled. He was proud of his world and the changes that had been made there after its times of troubles. He touched Joey's and Leigh's arms and started to tell them about the history of his world.

"We were once like your world is now, so much hate and greed. Our people at that time were destroying this world, and we didn't see anything wrong with that. We fought almost continuous wars with each other over small things. Millions of us were killed."

Joey and Leigh were awestruck by this information. How had these people been able to change their ways so radically? This world was a shining example of peace and universal love. Yet Arnor was telling them that at one time, it had been just like Earth.

Arnor continued with his narration, "Our planet was so polluted that we had hundreds of species of animals that were going extinct. We were killing ourselves and everything else here with us. On an interesting note, we had a small number of people who were trying to change our way of thinking. They were telling us that we should think of love and peace and not greed, fighting, wars, hate, and fear. We were telling them to shut up and wake up, that this was how it was supposed to be, all business and manufactured pleasure. We were so shocked on that day when our visitors arrived with the messages that changed everything here for us."

CHAPTER FOURTEEN

Their living quarters at the visitors' residence were like those of an expensive large hotel in some major city on Earth—very large, with a living room, a large bath, two bedrooms. It was more like a suite.

There was a being there to help them. He was like one of the large grizzly bears. He spoke to them in a voice like a rumbling bass drum, "My name is Ronod. I am here to assist you both with whatever you need. I will be here for you all of the time that you are here until you leave this world. Please call on me for any help that you may need."

Leigh said, "Thank you, kind Sir, for your help."

Joey and Leigh took the time to rest. Later, they got cleaned up and changed into clean clothes. They spent some time just looking out of their high windows at the city scene while talking over their first impressions of this world. Much of it looked like any Earth city, until they looked closer. It was so clean and well-kept. It was obvious that the people here took pride in their environment, and that showed. There were no sounds of sirens moving through the streets. There were no street people shuffling around, trying to find a meal and a place to spend the night. There were no signs of big money moving things around for their own profit while ignoring the poverty on the sidewalks.

As they talked, they both came to the decision that this wouldn't be a bad place to live. The door chime sounded. Leigh said, "Computer, open the door."

It was a similar system. It worked here as well. In walked Mr. Savak and Lieutenant Mara. They were both dressed in full uniforms.

Joey murmured to Leigh, "Boy, they look good together, like a couple."

Leigh nodded her head in agreement.

Mr. Savak said, "Joey, Leigh, if you are ready, we can all go downstairs to this dinner. Please, both of you, try to remember, you are the guests of honor here. Please just be yourselves. You have nothing to worry about. These people have never met an Earth person before, so they have no preconceived idea of what you will be like. Just be yourselves. Shall we go now?"

The lift system was again similar to the one on the *Universal Peace*. They went down and exited it on the main floor. They were greeted by a large crowd of beings that overflowed the dining hall. Everyone was smiling and welcoming them.

Once inside the dining hall, they were escorted to a large table at one end of the room facing the rest of the hall. Sitting down, they found themselves beside the chairman of the Combined Worlds Administration. Everyone was chatting with one another. Joey looked past to the other side of the chairman, and he saw Arnor sitting there. Sitting on the other side of Leigh was Lieutenant Mara, and beside her was Mr. Savak. He saw Josa and Dr. Bara sitting near Captain Arnor.

Chairman Omana turned slightly to Joey and said, "Earthman Joey, I have sensed that I might have said something this afternoon that might have worried you, when I said that we were rethinking our plans for your world.

"Please, Joey, let me tell you now that Earth has nothing to fear from us. Please wait until we are having our meeting before you make a decision about this. You have nothing at all to worry about. Our culture does not go around conquering other worlds. That is not how we work. We are a peaceful culture. We do not practice war."

He then nodded to someone off in one corner of the room. The room quickly became quiet. Omana stood up and started speaking to the entire room, "May I have everyone's attention, please?"

When there was complete quiet, he said, "Thank you all. My brothers and sisters from all of our Combined Worlds, we are here this evening to welcome into our midst two visitors from that far-off world known as Earth. These people have come here as our guests. They have come here willingly and openly. We welcome them. Some of you have already heard of their actions on board the *Universal Peace*. They have displayed that behavior that we all promote: loving kindness and the desire to reach out to help others. I am greatly honored to have beside me at this table these two Earth people representatives. I present to you all, from the planet Earth, Joey and his life partner, Leigh. Please give them your welcome."

The hall erupted into applause and cheers. Joey and Leigh were both very embarrassed as they stood up to be honored.

Chairman Omana waited a few moments for the cheering to subside. He thanked the crowd and then waved them back into their seats. The waitstaff quickly began serving the food to the diners. The food was excellent. Joey and Leigh saw that it was almost all-vegetarian. There was a little fish served.

As they were eating, Chairman Omana told them that he was excited to hear about what life was like on Earth and what they thought about his culture so far. Joey and Leigh enjoyed the light chatter. It continued steadily for a few hours. The dinner finished up, and everyone returned to their rooms.

Joey and Leigh slept well that night.

The next morning, after breakfast, they were guided to a nearby office building that housed the Combined Worlds Administration Headquarters. They were again impressed with how clean everything was and how courteous everyone was. Even the people walking past them on the street were all friendly.

Upstairs in the building, they were taken to a conference room. They were starting to become familiar with having their friends from the ship with them at these meetings. Sitting down at the conference table and sipping some hot tea, they were greeted by everyone. When Omana entered and sat down, the idle chatter stopped, and the meeting began.

Omana started the meeting with "Joey, Leigh, thank you for being here this morning. First, let me tell you both a little bit about us, our world, and our culture. Please have patience with me for a few minutes. I don't know how much that you have been told so far, so I will tell this to you from the start. This world that you are on is not the first world of our culture. That world is near here. I understand that Captain Arnor is requesting that he be able to take you there after you leave here. I am going to tell him yes, he can. Mr. Savak and I are from the same world. As is your friend, Lieutenant Mara. We are an ancient culture that dates back for more than three hundred thousand of your Earth years. We have evolved a great distance from those early times.

"At one time, we were a fierce, warlike world. We lived that warrior lifestyle of conquering everything that we saw as desirable or as a threat. Our culture was doomed to self-destruction. It was like all worlds that use violence as a means to an end. We lived with that hate-fear-greed mentality. That is the downward spiral toward that a self-destructive end, cultural suicide on a world-class scale.

"One day, our world was given a gift of sight. We were shown that what we were doing with ourselves and with our world was taking us to oblivion. We received that message of enlightenment from that Great Spirit guide, who works to lead us all toward the good, toward the light, and away from the darkness. For the first time, we saw that spiritual path that would lead us upwards and not downwards.

"Joey, Leigh, we struggled for a long time with this change. But eventually, and please know that it took us more than three hundred of your years to make the change. We changed for the better. Our evolving continues to this day. We have become a culture that reaches out and helps others. We teach peace and universal love for all beings everywhere. We bring our messages of this Path of Peace to other worlds, and then we watch them for their process of evolving."

Joey glanced around and saw his friends were listening with misty eyes and with nods of their heads in agreement at what was being said. He also noticed that they were watching the chairman with that same look that he had seen on the faces of those humans who had sat with and listened to the Dalai Lama—that special look on the face of someone who is in the presence of a great spiritual Leader.

He turned his attention back to the chairman, who had a small smile on his face while watching Joey.

"We have become role models for many other worlds. Today, we have welcomed more than thirty other worlds into our combined culture. We have worked to introduce them to our messages of peace and love for all. And we have assisted them in moving forward on this, what we like to call, the Path of Peace.

"We watch many, many other worlds that are in the various stages of evolution and growth. Our attention is drawn to certain worlds when we sense that their cultures begin to show signs of intelligence, when they begin to evolve themselves with the sciences and collective mechanical abilities. We listen for those worlds that start to show widespread communications between themselves.

"When we see or detect these signs, then we carefully move closer and watch them for a while further. We are very careful to not let them see us at first. We don't want to frighten them. Fear is not what we are hoping to promote. We then chose certain individuals on these worlds that we see as showing promise in their evolving. We sit with them sometimes in their sleep. Sometimes, we bring them to us for short visits. We teach them about the Path of Peace. We help them as much as we can.

"Joey, Leigh, we have been watching your world for some time now. We visited your world many thousands of your years ago. We were working with your species and bringing them along the path. I was a small part of that effort and was very interested in how it was progressing. Then the accident happened. *Celestial Explorer* was struck by a meteor, and the crash destroyed her and caused a shift in your planet's crust. In our fear and confusion, we made a mistake. We ran away from your world because we thought that it might explode. We should have stayed nearby to check for survivors, but we didn't. What we didn't find out about, until much later, was that there were survivors, some from your world and some from our ship. They were scattered all over your world, but they survived. And your species survived in scattered groups around your world. Those small groups became the forerunners of your species today. It would be eleven thousand of your years later before we detected signs that those survivors had stayed alive long enough to start myths, legends, and concepts. They worked for the hope that your species would begin their evolving again. Two thousand of your years ago, we contacted a few of your species again to try to start the process again, but we had very little luck with our efforts. Those that we did teach, in turn, taught others, but their lessons became twisted and distorted, until they no longer were working toward evolution. Instead, they had become causes for self-centered egos, greed, fear, and hate."

The conversation had become very intense. Omana smiled.

Arnor spoke up, saying, "Sir, perhaps we can continue this discussion in a quieter setting. Joey, do you mind if we use your room to finish this meeting?"

"No, Sir. Let's go."

The small group, being led by Joey and Omana, headed into the hallway, back outdoors and back to the vehicles to transport them all back to their residence. Twenty minutes later, they were all sitting in Joey and Leigh's room: Omana, Joey, Leigh, Arnor, Dr. Bara, Mr. Savak, Lieutenant Mara, and a few other members of Omana's staff.

Everyone had grouped the chairs and sofa into a rough circle shape. Cups of hot tea and glasses of water filled everyone's hands. Omana waited until everyone was settled in a little. He looked around for nods of approval. He continued, "Joey, Leigh, to finish what I was saying about your world, about one hundred of your years ago, we noticed that your species was starting to stretch outward from your planet. So we moved closer and were shocked at what we heard from your species communications signals. It seems that your species was dancing on that thin edge of complete destruction of yourselves and your planet. Our survey vessels were met with overwhelming fear and weapons. Some of our people were killed. And one or two of our people reacted strongly. The decision was made here that we would isolate your species to its own world. We would move to confine it to its own isolated area of negativity. Your species had already sent probes outward toward the edges of your sun's system. We could not let any of them beyond that point. We could not let your dark, infectious, negative, destructive behavior leak out beyond your own solar system."

Joey leaned forward as he started to get ready to interject something, when he felt Leigh's hand on his arm gently sending him the message to hold back for a few more minutes.

Omana continued to speak, "As we moved in a little closer to your world, we started to see something else that we hadn't anticipated. We saw and sensed a slowly growing movement of your beings who were becoming enlightened. We have watched as many of them stood up and spoke out about believing in peace and love. We saw some people like the human Gandhi, the man Nelson Mandela, the woman Mother Theresa. There have been many others too. We listened to the writings of the man known as John Lennon. We watched and spoke with the man known as Buddha. We began to watch these people as others listened to them and were changed to positive-thinking humans. We were encouraged to wait and see.

"Joey, we decided to select two people who showed great promise and to contact them and to bring them here to meet with us. We wanted to talk to them while they were here on our world. There were two people who caught our attention because of their personal journeys and their evolving behavior. Our thoughts were that once we were able to talk to them here, then we would decide what to do with your world based on the answers that these humans gave us.

"Joey, you and your life partner, Leigh, are those two humans."

Chapter Fifteen

At this moment, Joey felt like that old quote "He had the weight of the world on his shoulders." Again, he started to say something, but he saw that Omana wanted to continue, so he let him.

"Joey, Leigh, you two have rocked our beliefs about your world backwards a little. When you two agreed to travel here, you gained our attention. But later on, the work that you two began to do with the crew members on *Universal Peace* forced us to reconsider our opinions about your world and its peoples. If you two are an example of this new growing movement on your world toward peace and universal love, then we will have to reexamine our thoughts.

"But then, you did something that set us back into our collective seats even further. I am speaking about the incident with the crewman Jaco. Only an enlightened and aware person would even consider doing what you did to him in response to his attack on you. We want to thank you for that, and because of that, we want to welcome you into our culture. You have proven yourself as someone who believes in the Path of Peace.

"And you, Leigh, you also have proven yourself to us. Your work and your skills as a healer have been reported to us by Dr. Bara. Your willingness to help other peoples without regard for their species—these are just the types of behaviors that we look for in those peoples that we contact. Your teaching us about this thing that you call hugs—this is something new to us, and we are finding out that doing it just makes us feel good.

"Both of you have caused us to reconsider our thoughts about your world. What we would like to do now, if you two are willing to do this for us, is to send you both back home as teachers of what we practice. We would like you two to go home and tell other Earth people about our Path of Peace. We will continue to watch your people and to contact those whom we see as becoming evolved. If your world begins to change and to move toward the peaceful path, then we will, at some time in the near future, reveal ourselves and make open contact. We will then guide your world onto the path until it can evolve to that point where it can become a member of our Combined Worlds Administration."

Joey and Leigh were dumbstruck. They didn't know what to say. Listening to Omana as he had spoken, they had rolled through a wide range of emotions. Confusion changed to anger, which changed to fear, and then it all changed to awe. And now he had just offered them a chance to work for him and the worlds that he represented. They were being asked to do all this by returning home to Earth and working for peace.

Omana was watching their faces and the changes in their emotions. He spoke to them again, "Joey, Leigh, this is a very important task for you both. Will you both please do me one favor? Will you both *not* make your decision right now? Please take a few days to think this over. Visit this world, and meet some of our people. I understand that there are many people who want to meet you two. We can meet again in a few days' time from now. We can talk. You both can give me your decision then. I want to thank you both for doing what you are doing and for what you have already given us."

They all stood up to get ready to leave the room. Leigh moved over to stand in front of Omana as he turned toward the door. She softly said, "Sir."

He stood in front of her, looking into her eyes. Slowly, a smile grew on his face. With his psychic sense, he knew what was coming. Leigh stepped forward to him, and reaching her arms around him, she gave him a hug. Her murmured "Thank you" was barely audible.

Everyone broke out into big smiles.

A short time later, after Joey and Leigh had returned to their quarters and changed clothes, they met Arnor and his crew members outside the residence building. Everyone bundled into a waiting vehicle. Arnor was driving. He slowly moved up and away, toward the north, away from the city. The broad smile on his face was a hint about where they were headed.

They flew for a few hours. As they entered an area of very large farms, Arnor began to slow down and to descend. Joey watched as they headed toward a cluster of farm buildings located at the beginning of a small, shallow valley that slowly descended from the mountains. They heard Arnor speak into a communications device.

"Upland farm. Upland farm. This is Arnor. I am descending to your landing area. I have six friends on board. We are here to visit. Can we join you for dinner?"

The response came quickly in a woman's voice, "Arnor, it's about time that you got here. We were expecting you three hours ago. What took you so long? Huh! Probably sitting somewhere and talking. Of course, you will stay for dinner and for the night too. Don't you try to talk your way out of this. You have been away for a long time on this mission. Now you are home."

Arnor was smiling broadly. This woman was his mother. And she still told him where to go and what to do.

The landing was soft. As they all stepped out of the vehicle, they were met by an energetic elderly woman dressed in farmer's work clothes, accompanied by a mixed small group of people. The joyful chatter was a delight to hear. Arnor guided Joey and Leigh to the front facing the incoming group.

"Joey, Leigh, this wonderful woman is my mother, Isis. This is my sister, Ariana. My brother, Ardth. And these are their spouses."

Joey and Leigh laughed and said, "Hi."

The woman Isis looked at them all and nodded her head at everyone. It seemed that she was very familiar with all the ship's crew.

"Come with me now. We can go to the house. The three-fifteen rain shower is due in a few minutes. There is no need for us to stand around out here and get wet."

Once they were all at the house and standing on the porch of this old farmhouse, memories for both Joey and Leigh were stirred up. They had been in similar places near their home in Maine. Like all old farm homes, this one seemed to generate laughter from whoever was there. Joey was watching, when about ten minutes later, the sky rapidly clouded over and opened up. There was a brief, heavy downpour that lasted for fifteen minutes. The sky quickly cleared up again, and the sun was shining brightly again. By this time, they were all sitting in chairs on the porch. Isis had provided them with mugs of hot tea. Joey thought that it tasted like a chai tea, one of his favorites.

Isis turned toward Joey and Leigh. "Thank you both for coming to see us. We have been itching to meet you ever since we heard about you coming here to our world with Arnor."

Leigh smiled. "Thank you. This is a wonderful surprise for us. We haven't really been on a set schedule since we first boarded Arnor's ship. Your home is so beautiful. I grew up near some large farms. Please tell us a little about this one. What do you raise? How large is it? I don't see many workers. Do you do this all yourself?"

Isis smiled back at her. She was obviously very proud of her farm. "We have one of the oldest farms in this area. Our family has been here for more than twenty thousand years. We have . . .," she turned to Arnor and said, "How can this be translated into their world's terms?"

He chuckled and answered, "Leigh, our farm covers more than one thousand of your Earth's square miles."

Isis smiled in thanks to him. "We have more than one hundred workers. Our growing seasons are different from your Earth ones. Our crops are mostly vegetables. Our world does very little meat. We have a lot of fish and some birds that we grow for meat. Most of our world's nutrition comes from our vegetables. We work very closely with our world's ecosystem. We learned long ago to treasure it. Today, we work to benefit it and to keep it alive and well. On your world, do you do this also?"

Joey and Leigh were embarrassed to answer her.

Arnor interjected, "Mother, that is one reason why we have carried them here—so that we can take them back to their world with our messages about all of this."

Isis looked at them and just nodded her head in understanding.

She looked at Leigh a little more intensely. Her face changed into a look of surprise. She blurted out, "Leigh, you are with child! Arnor, how can you make her dress in those clothes? She needs something much looser. Leigh, you will come with me right now. I can help you with this problem." Taking Leigh firmly by her arm and giving everyone else a harrumph of indignation toward them all, she led Leigh off into the house while making a steady chatter of woman-to-pregnant-woman conversation.

Everyone there all just smiled and kept quiet for a moment. Then Joey spoke to Arnor, "Captain, I don't know if you know this or not, but as a younger man, I worked part-time on some dairy farms. I would love to see this farm."

Arnor broke out into a big smile. "Joey, we have been watching you and Leigh for a long time. We saw you working as a younger man. That's one reason why I brought you both here. I knew that you would feel at home."

Joey sat back in his seat. He had forgotten that this culture had the ability to move backward or forward in time. He was surprised to hear that they had been interested in him for such a long period of time.

Arnor was starting to tell him about the farm's operations, when his sister, Ariana, stepped out from the doorway to the house.

"We have dinner prepared for everyone. Would you like to eat out here on the porch or inside at the table?"

It was quickly decided to do a self-serve meal, with everyone picking up their own dishes, and then they would eat outside on the porch. As they stepped into the house, they were assailed by the mouth-watering smells from the food that had been prepared for them.

As Joey was picking up his choices of foods, he heard the room fall into silence behind him. Turning quickly, he was struck by a vision. He would remember this scene fondly for the rest of his life.

There stood Leigh at the foot of the stairs leading to the upstairs of the house. She was stunning in a loose-fitting dress of light blues and greens that fell to her midcalf area, with that special glow from her pregnancy that seemed to just radiate from her body like a soft light, this special radiance that he was getting used to now. Her hair had been combed out, and Isis had even provided her with some beautiful jewelry. Joey's private thought was *Wow! I thought that I loved her before, but this makes her a goddess for me.*

His reverie was broken by the gentle sounds of hands clapping from around the room. His face went pink, and it was matched by Leigh's face. Later, they would share with each other how much they both were coming to love these people.

The meal became an excited, animated chatter between everyone. Toward the end of the meal, they were all treated to the view of a magnificent sunset over the nearby mountain valleys. The clear air with the colors of the reds, oranges, greens, and yellows in the clouds—it left them all with a sense of deep inner peace.

Still later, with the slowly encroaching darkness and a slight chill coming to the air, they all began to drift indoors.

A short time later, it seemed that everyone was politely stifling yawns. Isis, looking around the room, saw this and said, "That's it. Everyone is tired—and with good reason. Why don't you all go to bed and get some rest? We can talk some more in the morning."

Joey and Leigh were told to take an upstairs bedroom. As they were saying good night, he noticed that Savak and Mara were quietly walking together. They were moving slowly up the stairs together to another bedroom. Joey's thoughts were *Oh, that's good for them. They fit so well together.*

Arnor and Bara were staying downstairs. Isis was ecstatic about having everyone stay the night. This old farmhouse was like a lot of old farmhouses everywhere. It was familiar to being the host to extra overnighters. One of Joey's last thoughts as he drifted off to sleep was how much this place felt like a home. And the warmth of Leigh's body next to him was so nice. *Hmmmm.*

CHAPTER SIXTEEN

The murmur of voices in the background, the sounds of movements throughout the house, the occasional rattle of pots and pans from the kitchen beneath them—Joey and Leigh were slowly coming awake to these sensations. And then there was that mouth-watering smell of cooking from the kitchen.

Joey was thinking, *What a wake-up call. None better anywhere.*

Opening his eyes and peeking at the window, he saw that it was just starting to get light out. Then he remembered. This was a working farm, and "Up with the sun; down with the sun" was the norm.

As he shifted his weight, Leigh turned to him, and opening her eyes, she smiled at him.

"I was wondering how long it would take you to wake up, sleepyhead."

She slid sideways into the contours of his body and moaned a little. Her hands started to wander over his body.

Joey started to react at once. Then he stopped. "What about . . . ?"

Leigh smiled and murmured, "No problem, my hero. What's to worry about? No, you can't harm the baby. It's too early with all of this. Trust me, my love. And besides . . ."

She moved her body over and on top of his, shifting slightly. Her lips sought out his, and he welcomed her deep, soul-searching kiss. His arms and hands began to caress her body. His thought was *God, how I love her.*

They made love together softly, gently. Joey was becoming very conscious about that growing swelling in her lower abdomen. He murmured, "Love you, my huckleberry friend."

"Love you, my hero."

Later, there was a quiet knock on the door. Isis's voice came through quietly. "If you two are awake, breakfast is about to go onto the table."

Joey answered her quickly, "Thank you. We have been watching the beauty of your farm."

Leigh poked him in the ribs with her elbow. She said, "We'll be right there, Isis. We overslept a little."

Isis's voice came through the door again with an almost-visible smile at their comment. "Sure, whatever you say. Breakfast is ready."

When they came downstairs to breakfast, they were greeted by a table laden with food, with their friends, old and new, bustling about the dining room and kitchen. There seemed to be a continuous stream of happy chatter and laughter from everyone.

Ardth asked them both if they would like to take a short tour of the farm. Arnor nodded his head to them.

After they all finished breakfast, Joey, Leigh, Arnor, Mara, and Savak boarded a strange-looking vehicle driven by Ardth.

Slowly taking flight, they were flown around the fields and boundaries of the farm. Joey was astounded by both the size of it and the types of machinery that were being used to do the work. At one location, Ardth landed, and Joey had a chance to sit in the control cabin of a very interesting, very large farming machine. He felt like he was in heaven. He had always had a special affinity for operating heavy equipment. This one was designed to do the work, and it could fly from place to place. The operator was one of those beings who looked like a large grizzly bear. His voice was a deep rumble. But he watched for a few moments as Joey sat the controls. He and Joey hit it off immediately. Within a few minutes, they were chattering back and forth like old friends who hadn't seen each other in a while. They talked about comparing notes on equipment that they each had operated and loved. Everyone else just stood back and watched with broad smiles on their faces.

In the early afternoon, they stopped at the top of a large hill overlooking the forested mountainsides and a large stream. Here they ate a lunch that Isis had packed for them before they had left that morning. Joey and Leigh were again amazed at the stunning beauty of the area. The valley floor was covered with farm fields. There was a medium-sized stream that flowed down from one of the mountainsides, bubbling and meandering in its route, to a distant sea. Those stunning mountains around them, the bright-blue sky with its slowly moving scattering of puffy white clouds, and that sense of ancient peace that seemed to rise out of the very soil around them (even the scattered wild creatures that they saw seemed to have no reason to be wary of these beings who were watching them)—there was a sense that everyone shared this world equally.

In midafternoon, Arnor brought them back to the house. They were expected back in the city that evening. Isis took Leigh by the arm again, speaking in her "I'm the queen bee on this farm" voice, saying, "Come with me, Leigh. And don't you argue with me either."

Leigh smiled and went with her. Everyone began packing up their clothing and things. Arnor was talking to his brother and sister. A few minutes later, Leigh returned with Isis. Her eyes were wet with tears. Joey hurried to her side.

"Are you OK? What's wrong?"

She nodded her head. "Isis just gave me . . ."

Isis spoke up, "A woman needs some real clothes that fit her and not just those uniform things all the time. That's something that you men don't always understand."

Leigh held up a large travel bag filled with clothes similar to the dress that she had worn the evening before. Joey's eyes started to fill with tears. Turning to Isis, he murmured, "I owe you so much. Thank you, Isis. You and your family have done so much for us. I will remember you all for the love that you have given us."

He stepped closer to her. Arnor and his crew knew what was coming. They just smiled and waited to see what her reaction would be. They were pleasantly surprised.

Joey opened his arms, and placing them around her, he gave her a long hug. She quickly accepted it and hugged him in return. Drawing back a little, Joey told her, "You and your family are like a family for me. If it's all right with all of you, I just want to say to you all that I love you all."

They had walked outside. Isis and her family were wishing them all farewell. They had climbed back aboard the vessel that they had arrived in for the trip back to the city. Arnor was driving. Lifting off slowly, they headed back around the mountains and toward the late-afternoon sun.

Arnor called out to Joey and asked him to sit in the copilot's seat beside him. He began to show Joey the controls to operate the vehicle. He told Joey that what he had seen when Joey was talking to the equipment operator on the farm had impressed him. He felt that Joey might, with some training, be able to operate some of the vehicles here. Joey focused on what he was being taught. Arnor even had him try the controls for a short time.

Leigh watched and smiled. Joey was at home with these kinds of things. Out of the corner of her eye, she watched as Savak and Mara sat very close together. Savak's arm slowly reached up and around Mara's shoulders. Her head leaned into his shoulder. Nothing was said. But it was obvious what had slowly come to be. Leigh just smiled in joy for them both.

Back at the residence building, everyone went back to their rooms. Joey and Leigh had talked to the others, and they all agreed to take him and Leigh for a walking tour of the downtown area that evening.

A short time later, they started out. Arnor and Bara were leading the way. As they walked, Arnor told them about his city. The pride in his voice was obvious. He pointed out various buildings and explained their purpose. As they were walking past some shops and restaurants, suddenly, Arnor said, "Let's go in here. This place has great food." They all crowded into a small restaurant. He was right. The food was very good. The owner of the restaurant and Arnor obviously knew each other. When he found out whom Joey and Leigh were, he insisted and then argued with Arnor that there would be no bill for the food. Joey did something special. He told the owner that he would sign his signature to a large piece of paperlike material. The owner could then place it in his display case as a sign that the people from Earth had eaten there.

As they were walking back to the residence building, Joey asked Arnor, "Captain, the people who have lost their citizenship, where do they live? I haven't seen anyone here that looks like a panhandler like we have on Earth."

Arnor explained, "Joey, these people who have violated our rules about violence are all made to live outside the cities. Only citizens can be in the cities, although many of the noncitizens do apply for specialized programs that allow them to work to regain their citizenship. Some of them volunteer for our military forces, and after a set amount of service time, they can become citizens again. The owner of the restaurant where we just had dinner is such a man. He made a bad mistake many years ago. He volunteered to serve in our military. He was under my command. When he regained his citizenship, he returned here, and I helped him to get started in his restaurant. We have remained friends ever since. Our world is such that even those who harm others can, if they want to do the necessary work, rebuild their lives and become welcomed citizens again. But they have to want to do this. They have to want to do the necessary work to make it happen."

Back at the residence building and settling in for the night, Joey and Leigh sat for a few hours looking out of the windows and quietly talked. They both had mixed feelings about this world. On one hand, they would like to stay here to live, perhaps even to spend the rest of their lives here. *But* they also were a little homesick for Earth and their friends there that they had known for years.

The next morning, they were told to be at another meeting with Omana. It would be held in the Combined Worlds Administration building. After breakfast, they dressed and met the ship's crew outside. A short flight across a few city blocks, and they were there again, upstairs and into a small conference room. They were seated. Omana smiled at them.

"Has your visit with us been an enjoyable one? Captain Arnor has spoken to me about your visit to one of our farms yesterday.

"Leigh, your beauty adds to this room."

Joey answered him, "Sir, we are in love with your world. It is such a beautiful place. And the people here are so nice."

Omana smiled. "Thank you both. We are all proud of our home worlds and what they have come to represent. We here, on this world, are at the center of our Combined Worlds. Our worlds number more than thirty. We all act as partners in our efforts at peace and universal brotherhood among everyone."

His face took on a serious note. "Joey, Leigh, have you had time to reflect upon my request of you both?

"We have had numerous contacts with your world for many thousands of your years. Our vessels have been fired upon by your military. They have had attempted crashes by your military aircraft. Our representatives have been chased by people from your Earth. That is not how we want to be regarded. Not as something to be feared but as friends.

"We have decided to try this different way of making contact—by bringing you both here and showing you what our world is like. We are hoping that this will open the door to further contact between us. We would like to be able to open the door to your world so that we can begin to teach all of you the way of the path to peace. We hope that you two can return to your world and carry the message of who and what we are to those others on your world who would be open to our way of living. We eventually would like to be able to include your world in our Combined Worlds culture.

"I ask you both again. Will you two help us with this hope and dream that we have for your world? If we cannot do this, then we will have to isolate your world to prevent it from contaminating other worlds with the beliefs that they have now. Those things like fear, hate, greed, and violence—we cannot let these things escape into the surrounding solar systems near you."

Leigh reached out and grasped Joey's hand. She squeezed it tightly and then relaxed her hand. Her message to him was clear. Joey looked at Omana.

"Sir, we have come to admire and to love all of the people here that we have met. What you teach and how you believe are so powerful. Sir, yes, Sir! We will do what you ask of us. But there is one request that we want you to grant us first."

Omana looked surprised, but he stared at Joey intently. He was puzzled that his personal intuition had not told him about this part of the conversation. It usually never failed him. Hmm. That made him curious.

"Yes. What do you want from me?"

Joey looked at Leigh.

She nodded her head in agreement with him. She smiled at him.

Joey looked at Omana again. "Sir, if we can do this work for you . . . Well, Sir, we want your promise that we can return here at some time to live for a while here on this world. Sir, we have come to love this world."

Omana sat back in his seat with a surprised look on his face. Then his face broke out into a slowly growing smile.

"Joey, Leigh, you both have my promise on this. I would be very happy to have you both living here on this world."

CHAPTER SEVENTEEN

That afternoon, they all had the chance to get some rest. The excitement among them was almost visible. This part of their work was finished. They were all starting to itch to get back into space and underway again. Joey knew this feeling well from his experience as a young man on ships at sea.

Arnor had come to see them and informed them that they all had to leave shortly to return to the ship. But first, they were going to a party for the crew members' families who lived on this world. It was going to be at the landing port. After the party, they would reboard the shuttle and return to *Universal Peace.*

They packed their clothing and said their good-byes. As they arrived at the landing port, they entered the primary building. They were introduced to a small crowd of people. These then were the families of the crew members from *Universal Peace* who were from this world. They had come to see them. This group of beings numbered about 250. Arnor guided Joey and Leigh to the front of the crowd.

"Hello, everyone. I would like you to meet Joey and Leigh. They are from a world named Earth. They have come here with us to both see our world and to meet with the chairman of the Combined Worlds Administration. These are very special people. Please welcome them."

The applause was instant. Joey and Leigh found themselves besieged with well-wishers. After a short while, Joey stepped back and to one side. Looking around, he saw a small group of people with somber faces standing off to one side in a corner. Touching Arnor's arm, he nodded to them. Arnor's face grew solemn. He made an internal decision. Taking Joey with him, he walked across the room to this small group.

Standing in front of them, he said, "Joey, these people are the family members of Jaco."

Joey stepped forward slightly and introduced himself to them.

One of the men in the group spoke up quickly, "Captain Arnor, thank you for doing this. We were not sure if we should be here or not. Earthman Joey, we are the remaining members of the family of the man that you know as Jaco. We have been told by him all that took place on board your ship, including what you did for him. We want to say thank you so much for being one of the enlightened people. What you did is very powerful. We will hold your memory in our hearts forever. Thank you so much, kind Sir."

Joey spoke in a quiet voice, "I thank you all for coming here today to meet me. Please understand. I have made my share of bad decisions in my lifetime. Some of them caused harm to other people. I treated Jaco just like I would like to be treated if I make a bad choice. I think that he is a good man who just made a bad choice. Now, let's all put this behind us once and for all."

The man smiled. The others all had tears in their eyes. Joey stepped a little closer to the man. The man had a wary look on his face now. He looked at Arnor, who nodded his head in a silent approval of what he knew was to come. Joey opened his arms and hugged the man, who, with a surprised look on his face that quickly changed into a smile, visibly relaxed. Within the next few minutes, everyone in the group had been introduced to this Earth thing called hugs.

Arnor glanced at his wrist device and spoke out loudly to everyone in the room, "OK, everyone. Let's get on board the shuttle. We have to get back aboard *Universal Peace* quickly. We have another world to get to."

A short time later, when the shuttle was en route to the ship, Joey leaned against Leigh, and they shared what had happened.

Back on board, Arnor quickly became Captain Arnor again. "All right, everyone. We are scheduled to be at Mr. Savak's home world in ten days. Let's get underway now. All hands, get ready to get underway! Engineering, are you ready? Detectors, are you all set? Shields, are you all set?

"Captain to all hands. We are getting underway now. *Universal Peace* to all ships in this area. We are getting underway. Leaving Sirius Prime and heading for Lotus."

The bustling activity signaled that they were moving out into space again. Everyone on board shared that feeling: "This is where I'm meant to be, on a ship moving outward, maybe toward something new and exciting."

Leigh had headed to their quarters to change into her uniform. As she did so, she thought that she was going to have to start altering her clothing now or just start wearing the clothing that Isis had given her. That memory started her into tears again. What she had for uniforms was starting to get a little too snug. Joey changed into his work clothes, and as he hurried toward the engineering section, his wrist communicator beeped a message.

"Crewman Joey, please report to the bridge."

Now what is going on? he thought as he spun around in place and headed to the nearest lift station.

Leigh entered the health-care station. Dr. Bara had also just arrived. There were three crewmen with minor injuries waiting. Bara looked at Leigh and said, "If you can take care of this man with a cut on the right arm, I'll start with this one. It looks like he has a severe strain in his back muscles. That third crewman has a minor wound. She can wait for a little bit."

Leigh grabbed for some dressing material to start cleaning the wound site. Bara was smiling as he spoke to her, "That was a great time off on the surface. Did you enjoy meeting everyone there?"

"Oh yes. And Isis is a really special woman." She smiled with her recent memories of that family.

Joey entered the bridge area. Everyone was busy as *Universal Peace* started to move and to maneuver out of her parking orbit.

Arnor turned his head to look at Joey and said, "It seems like I am always thanking you for things. Well, just for that, I'm going to make you come here to the bridge control station and to work here for a while. There are some things here that I would like to teach you. Is that all right with you?"

"Umm, sure, but I don't know anything about this type of work, Captain."

"Listen, Joey. I watched you at my mother's farm, use your natural talent for operating heavy equipment. You are good. *Universal Peace* is really a very large piece of heavy equipment. Why don't you try this for a little while and then decide if you want to keep up with it?"

"OK, Sir. Where do you want me to start?"

"Right here beside me for a bit, until you get a sense for where everything is located. Pull up a chair here." He indicated a space on his right-hand side.

Joey quickly moved into place. He noticed that most of the bridge crew had smiles on their faces at his being there.

"Joey, I'll start by telling you about the stations on the left side of the main screen and then work my way across to the right-hand side. Here on the far left is ship's communication systems. Next to that is our ship's sensor readings. They project out to about ten thousand measures, or about five thousand of your Earth miles. Next to that is . . ."

That evening, Joey told Leigh about what his day had been like and all the new things that he was learning. She told him about Bara starting to assign her duties like being an assistant doctor instead of a nursing assistant. It seemed that they were both going through more changes in their lives.

Nine days later.

Joey was showing his natural skills as a quick study. He was quickly picking up about the bridge duties. Now they were entering into the solar system for the world known as Lotus. Mr. Savak was acting a little unusual for him. He was usually very composed and a rock with his emotions. Lately, he had become nervous and frequently very preoccupied. They were approaching his home world. He was looking forward to seeing his family. But there was something else there too. He was very quiet about whatever it was that was working on him.

Then they were moving into orbit near an area on the planet's northern hemisphere.

"Bridge to all stations, let's keep on our toes here. Engineering, all engines to slow. Detectors, have you any other vessels in sensor range?"

"Yes, Captain. We have three other ships in stationary orbit just north of us. About one hundred measures away."

"OK. Thank you. Engineering, all stop! All back slow! Engineering, all stop! Captain to all hands, we are here at Lotus. There will be liberty for all crew members for this world." Leaning back in his chair, he exhaled a sigh. "Mr. Chara, deflectors off. Mr. Savak?"

"Yes, Captain."

"Will you be going ashore this evening? Or will you wait until tomorrow morning?"

"If you don't mind, Captain, I have some details to take care of with my family. I would like to go ashore this evening."

"Done, Sir. We'll meet you at your home tomorrow around midmorning. I would like very much to . . . Well, when this event of yours is completed, I would like to have Joey and Leigh meet with your family—and perhaps with your world's leader."

"Yes, Sir. Those were my thoughts also, Sir."

Joey was a little mystified when he heard this, but he felt no concerns.

Later that evening, he told Leigh that they would be meeting Savak's family tomorrow after some sort of event there. He told her that Arnor had said that he wanted them to meet the leader for this world. Joey murmured to himself, "Oh, well. This means that we'll have to get dressed up again." He turned to say something more to her. A smile broke out on his face. He saw that Leigh had begun to snore slightly.

Their shuttle came in for a soft landing at a midsize city area in one of the northern land areas on this world. As they had circled this world, Arnor pointed out to them that this world was a younger world with almost-all steep mountains. These were heavily forested on the lower slopes and almost bare rock above that. The people here were deeply spiritual beings. It was these people who had introduced this Path-of-Peace spirituality to the other worlds in their Combined Worlds Administration. This world had become the center of this belief system.

Exiting the shuttle, they were met with a small group of people. Arnor apparently knew them all well.

"Hello again, my friends. It is so good to see you all again." Turning to Joey and Leigh, he introduced them to the group. "Joey, Leigh, these people are some of the family members of Savak. They have come to meet us and to guide us to their home in the mountains near here. This man is Savak's brother, Saran."

Saran smiled as he was introduced. "We have been expecting you all. Savak was insistent on having you both here for this ceremony. Welcome to Lotus. If you would follow me, please. We have a vehicle waiting to return us to our family home."

They boarded a nearby flying vehicle, and Saran was the pilot. As they wound their way across the city and toward a mountain pass, he told them about this world and his people. They had been here on this world for more than three hundred thousand of Earth years. The mountains supplied them with heat, water, and clear air. This world was slightly closer to its sun. Because of this, their temperature was warmer then Earth's. The valley areas were farmed for vegetable-based foods. The population of this world was not that large. Many of their people who had been born, raised, and schooled here. They had moved away and now lived on other worlds. He told them about their spiritual system and what it had done for their people. Their system taught that everyone had spirit guides. These guides could teach you how to live at peace with everything. They practiced a system that taught them to work with the natural world, no matter where they lived. Their system taught that all living things were beings with spirits and that we should work with them and not abuse them or kill them for sport. The system taught that all beings could communicate among one another. All a person had to do was to learn the language of the other beings.

Their vehicle was now floating down onto a landing area on a high meadow looking out over a steep-sided valley toward other mountains. There was a cluster of nearby buildings that were connected to and built into the rock face behind them. Small gardens covered much of the rest of the meadow area. Everything was overlooked by rocky tall ledges that rose to great heights above them. These mountains were being gently caressed by the passing of slowly moving white clouds. A bright-blue sky outlined everything. There seemed to be a peaceful watchfulness from these great mountains, almost as if these great masses really were beings of a different form who looked down onto these small moving beings that lived such short lives on their lower slopes.

Bringing the vehicle to a slow stop, Saran opened the doors. With a broad smile on his face, he motioned Joey and Leigh to step out onto the ground. Joey and Leigh took a moment to look around the area. The beauty was breathtaking. It felt like the very ground beneath them was draining away from them any stressful feelings that they might have brought with themselves, leaving them with that sense of deep inner peace.

Saran turned to them and said, "Welcome to my family home. And thank you both for coming here to help us to celebrate my brother Savak's Ceremony of Life Partner with Mara."

CHAPTER EIGHTEEN

Joey and Leigh looked at each other and broke out into wide smiles. So that was what was going on. They had both suspected that there was some sort of relationship between Savak and Mara, but this . . . This was a wonderful surprise. And for them to be invited to attend. Wow.

Savak's family home reminded Joey of an old medieval castle on Earth. It was a huge compound of stone buildings that backed up to the massive cliffs. These were towering upward from the plateau in front, these stone abutments of multishades of gray color.

They would later find out that there was an extensive system of caves that extended from the buildings deep into the mountain. Some of these were used for a type of hydroponic gardening. Others were used for storage and even living quarters. They all were using a type of geothermal heating. Lighting was a system of mirrors that reflected the sunlight down shafts into the caverns.

At the same time, there was no sense of intimidation. Instead, it all seemed to radiate a strong sense of peace and serenity. Leigh was reminded of pictures that she had seen of ancient Buddhist monasteries from rural China. Those great stone edifices looking downward on small pools of rainbow-colored gardens and fields, all the while clinging to the sides of mountains and being cared for by peaceful people dressed in saffron-colored robes.

The group walked toward the main building. As they neared the doorway, a man stepped out to greet them. He was tall, wiry; he had a greenish tinge to his skin. Moving in an almost-fluid motion, he approached them. Arnor was smiling so warmly. This man was obviously an old friend.

Touching Joey's and Leigh's arms gently, he said, "Joey, Leigh, may I introduce you both to my old friend, Stock. He was on your world once and helped a man there.

"Stock, here are Joey and Leigh, from the world known as Earth."
The man gave them a gentle smile and, in a quiet, slightly gravel-sounding voice, spoke, "I am so pleased to meet you. My son Savak has told me much about you both. I thank you both for coming here to be present when my son and Mara become life partners. Perhaps we can talk afterwards. I would like to hear news from your world. I am curious about it and how things are there now. Could you all follow me, please? The ceremony is about to start in a few moments."

They all walked up a few steps and entered the main building through its front door. The doorway opened into a large room. The surprise for Joey and Leigh was the warmth and abundant lighting that seemed to come from multiple reflected mirrors bringing it down from the rooftops. The air was moving slightly and filled with the scents of flowers and herbs. At the far end of this room was a corridor leading off to the right. They all walked toward it. This corridor, in turn, took them into another very large room. This room was almost filled with people. Joey was reminded of its similarity to a large event center–type of space with a podium set up at the far end. Their small group was escorted down toward the front. Once there, Arnor excused himself and went to stand where Savak and Mara were standing, about twenty feet away, facing the podium. Savak turned and smiled warmly at seeing them and nodded his head in welcome. Leigh noticed that Mara was dressed in a gown. She thought to herself, *She looks stunning.* It was the first time that she had seen Mara in something other than a uniform.

Stock now placed Joey and Leigh within a small group of people. Excusing himself, he went to stand beside Savak.

The low murmur of conversation in the room suddenly became very hush. A well-dressed tall, thin man entered the room from a side doorway. He was dressed in a light-blue robe that was decorated with a variety of symbols. Joey was instantly aware of the sense of peace that seemed to emanate from him, almost like the flow of a gentle white light. This seemed to fill the area around him as he moved into the center of one end of the room. He stopped and stood in front of the podium, facing the small group there. Everyone had turned to watch him. He spoke in a quiet, gentle voice that seemed to carry outward to everyone. He motioned the group to gather in front of him. Savak and Mara were in the center, with Arnor standing to one side, and slightly behind was Savak. To Savak's right side was Mara, with a beautiful woman, who looked a little like Mara, standing just to her right side and slightly behind her. Behind Arnor stood Josa and Bara.

Savak turned suddenly to face Joey and Leigh. With a hurried motion from his left hand, he motioned Joey to come and to stand with Arnor and the others. Mara, looking at Leigh, made a similar motion to Leigh and indicated that she should stand beside her on her right side. Joey and Leigh were stunned.

"What to do? What do we do?"

Arnor now motioned to them both again and nodded his head toward them. "Please, it's all right. It's all right."

Joey and Leigh both looked at each other and walked forward. Savak smiled. Mara smiled. It was going to be all right.

The gentle man in the center smiled at them and began to speak, "I welcome you all to this celebration of the coming together of Savak and Mara as Life Partners. They are now pledging to remain together as life partners for the rest of this lifetime. They are taking the oath to support and to defend each other, to help each other, to care for each other, to nurture each other until their lives are finished for this lifetime.

"Savak, do you agree to these oaths as I have spoken them? Do you love, honor, and accept Mara as your life partner?"

Savak turned to Mara, and taking her hands in his, he looked deeply into her eyes and said, "Yes. I do love, honor, and gladly accept you as my life partner."

The spiritual leader turned slightly toward Mara, "Mara, do you agree to these oaths that I have spoken? Do you love, honor, and accept Savak as your life partner?"

Mara spoke with a voice that mirrored the flow of tears of love in her eyes, "Yes. I do love, honor, and accept you, Savak, as my life partner to be with me always."

The spiritual leader now placed his hands on Savak's and Mara's shoulders. He spoke in a raised voice to be heard by everyone there, "These two people are now joined together as one. Their minds, their bodies, their spirits are now together for this lifetime and for all future lifetimes. Let us all now show our joy for their joy."

Everyone in the room stood up and hollered out a cheer. Then the room erupted in a mob of people coming forward to congratulate the new couple. Joey and Leigh found themselves in a small huddle of friends that were in the center of a crowd of two hundred or more people.

After about twenty minutes, a loud voice was heard from the doorway at the front of the room. There, Stock was standing up on a small stool. He hollered out again, "Hey, everyone! Come on! Follow me, and we can have dinner now. Congratulations can be done while we're eating. Savak, Mara, come on. You two are the guests of honor for this."

Savak, while holding onto Mara's hand, was joined by Arnor, Bara, Josa, Joey, and Leigh. He led the way through the crowd until they were in the lead. They were also joined by the gentle man who had officiated at the ceremony. As they were walking toward Stock, Arnor did a quick introduction.

"Joey, Leigh, may I introduce you both to our great spiritual leader. This is Metaron. On our world, his name means *great soul*. Sir, this is Joey and Leigh from the world known as Earth. They are traveling with us on *Universal Peace*."

The gentle man was chuckling and trying to contain himself from a burst of outright laughter. Leigh noticed that his face reflected a deep happiness and that it bore deeply etched, well-used laughter lines. He spoke quickly to them, "I am so glad to meet you both. When this event is over, I would love to be able to spend some time talking to you both, perhaps in a quieter setting."

Then his laughter burst forth into a deep belly laugh that became instantly contagious to all who were nearby. It seemed that within seconds, the entire crowd was infected with this deep, raucous laughter. It all seemed to leave Joey and Leigh with a feeling of settled peacefulness. They were escorted into a large room that had been set up for dining. Everyone was quickly seated, and the meal was well received.

Later on, with slightly overfilled stomachs, Joey and Leigh were led back outside and walked toward their quarters in a nearby residential area of the compound. Nighttime had come, and they were awed by the stars in the sky and all the different star systems that were there. Arnor and Stock pointed out to them dozens of systems that they said were inhabited and known to the Combined Worlds Administration.

Arnor suddenly looked at one particular star. He got a serious, solemn look on his face. Turning to Stock, he said, "I very much want to take them to see Therma. I really think that they should be allowed to see it, to see what can happen to their world Earth. Do you think that I can have permission to do that?"

Stock looked back at him with a solemn, understanding look on his face. "Yes. I think that's a good idea. We can ask the leader if you can do that. I'm sure he will agree."

Joey and Leigh, listening to this exchange and starting to become used to the surprises from these men, weren't concerned. After being guided to their quarters, they quickly went to bed. Those full stomachs helped them get a good night's sleep.

The next morning, they were invited to eat with Savak's family and the ship's crew. They were seated with the spiritual leader. He was again chuckling. This seemed to be something that he did almost continuously. He said, "Well, you two earthlings. Now I can meet you formally. Heh. Heh. Heh.

"Hello. My name is Metaron. I am so happy to meet you both. I was on Earth once many, many years ago of your time. I met with and worked with some people there in a mountainous area with a very warm climate. I don't recall his name, but the human that I was teaching—well, he was a great student of my teachings.

"Arnor and his crew have kept me informed about your experiences on board his ship. Very interesting. It seems that you two are more evolved than I first thought.

"Leigh, your willingness to work in helping others to heal from their hurts, so wonderful of you. And these are people and even species that you have never encountered or have no connection to. Please listen to me carefully, Leigh. Your spirit guides have given a wonderful gift of healing to you. I strongly encourage you to use it, to learn more about it and from it. And this new life that you carry within you, oh, Leigh, what a gift for you for this time of your life.

"And you, Joey. Oh, Joey, you too carry something wonderful within you. You have a gift that many do not even know of. Your inner peace is one of the reasons that you were chosen for this trip to visit us here. What you did for the man Jaco, when I heard about that, I was in tears of joy for you. That act of forgiveness is what we are all about here in our culture. You have shown us that there are people on your world who are worth saving from your world's path of slow self-destruction. You two have shown us that there are still some surviving seeds of my teachings that are trying to blossom and to grow on your world. You two have made me so happy."

He suddenly erupted into laughter, mixed with tears of love and joy. Reaching out to them, he showed them that he remembered hugs.

All three of them were now wiping tears from their eyes. Metaron broke out into an uproar of laughter. Everyone caught that oh so easy-to-catch infection again, and the entire room was one large pool of laughter.

Moments later, after catching his breath, Metaron spoke to them again, saying, "Well, you two. We need to talk again later today. But I understand that Savak, Mara, Stock, and some others would like to take you around their home and to show you some of this world. I think that you both are already starting to sense why this world is our spiritual center. So go now. Join the others, and enjoy the day outside. We will meet again later today to continue our chat."

With another burst of laughter, he stood up, turned, and walked away.

Joey and Leigh stood up and left with Arnor and the ship's crew.

CHAPTER NINETEEN

As they walked across the compound toward the waiting shuttlecraft, Joey and Leigh noticed the exchanged looks and touches between Savak and Mara. Those gentle smiles. *Yes, these two were meant to be together as*, Leigh thought as she tried the phrase in her mind (it just sounded right), *life partners.*

Savak took the shuttle's controls, and Mara sat beside him as the copilot. The craft rose slowly into the air and moved away toward the valley beyond the compound. Savak and Mara began a narrative about their home world. It was obvious that they were so proud of it.

"Joey, Leigh, our world was once a place like your world Earth. It had started out as a beautiful place, full of wide plains and great bodies of water. There were animal species everywhere. Life was so abundant here. Then we began to fight, to kill each other and those other species that lived here. We raped the land of this world for its resources. We began to destroy it and ourselves. Our different peoples here were fighting and killing each other in senseless wars. We were using the excuse of our needs to kill our world. Our largest need was for weapons to destroy each other. We had killed off many of the other beings that inhabited this world with us. Our biggest product was hate, greed, fear, and paranoia. We had become a culture that believed in *us or them*, not in *we*. We had almost reached that point in our self-destruction when this whole world's ecosystem would come crashing down to finish us off once and for all."

Mara spoke up and added to the narrative, "This all was happening more than one hundred thousand of your years ago. Our people had always been warlike. We had brought ourselves to that point of complete destruction of everything here, including ourselves. Our soil was exhausted. Our water was badly polluted. Even our air was becoming poisonous to life forms. We had squandered our world's resources to the point where thousands of us were dying almost daily from the effects of our climate's deterioration.

"We finally reached the point where we learned that oh so important lesson: The only winners in warfare are those who make the weapons. Everyone and everything else loses.

"Then we experienced the miracle that started our path to salvage and our way back from the abyss that we were running toward. We had had, for some time, a few of our people who were speaking up about what was going on. But we treated them very badly. We persecuted them. We seized them and put them into confinement. We even had them killed.

"But they continued their speaking out about what we, as a culture, were denying and continuing to do to our world."

Savak began to speak again, this time with an excitement in his voice, "We were in great turmoil as a culture. Here we were, still doing business as usual and fighting off these people whom we felt just didn't understand about how to conduct a business culture.

"Then one person stepped forward. This person had the charisma to become a voice for change. We finally, finally began to listen. Later on, we would learn that this person had been in touch with beings from another world who wanted to help us to save ourselves from ourselves. This being from another world was guiding the man who had stepped forward with messages of hope for us and our world. The miracle that I spoke of was this man and his messages for us. Suddenly, some of our world's leaders began to listen to this man's messages. They began to change how they thought about our culture and what it was doing to our world.

"The change was slow at first. But it continued. We began to see the positive path ahead of us. The more that we saw the differences, the more that we started to work harder at it. This new leader became a spiritual leader for us. He taught us about peaceful coexistence, about learning how to live with our world as if it were another being that lived here, about our becoming a part of this world and not just some being that was living here and destroying it. He taught us how to think like *we* instead of like *us and them*.

"His teachings taught us how to become awakened and aware to all of those other things around us. His peacefulness became our dogma. We started to treat our world as our equal partner in life. Our awareness began to include those spirit guides, who are a valuable source of help for us all. They taught us about universal love between all beings everywhere, a universal brotherhood.

"Tomorrow, our spiritual leader will tell you more about this story. Right now, we are coming to the site of the home of the first leader who saved us all. Today, it is inhabited by a special being who, although not from this world, is the current incarnation of that first leader."

They passed over the end of a beautiful valley. They saw what seemed like hundreds of animals of different sizes. Some were similar to elk. Some were large and looked almost like buffalo. They noticed that none of these animals seemed to be afraid of their passage by them. Everything here seemed to radiate a sense of peace that was so strong that Joey thought that he could actually see it glittering in the air around them. They moved toward the end of the valley that nestled between two mountain peaks. There was so much green growth: trees, plants, grasses.

There at the end of the valley was a group of several buildings. They were built of stone and wood. They were well tended, and there seemed to be several humanoid figures around the buildings that were working at different tasks. The central building was large, like a community center.

After landing, they exited the shuttlecraft and walked toward the front of these buildings. There seemed to be a hushed quiet—not like that of trepidation, but more like that of a quiet, gentle peacefulness, similar to that which might be felt in some remote monastery.

As they strolled toward the buildings, the center door of the main building opened. Joey and Leigh were surprised at what emerged. The first sight of him put them on guard. The figure that stepped outside from the doorway and started to stroll toward them was not a humanoid.

What they saw was a very large tiger advancing toward them at a slow walking pace. He was colored like a Siberian tiger, white with black stripes. Arnor reached out and touched Joey. Joey jumped backward a little. At the same moment, Mara reached out and touched Leigh.

Arnor and Mara both murmured to them, "It's all right. Don't worry. There is no danger to you. This being is our oldest spiritual leader. He has been teaching us about peace for thousands of years."

As the tiger walked toward them, Joey was suddenly reminded of two memories from that time of his childhood. First was when he had visited a zoo. He had been fascinated by the tiger in a cage. He was overwhelmed by the beauty of the big cat as it paced from side to side of the cage, that rippling flow of muscles beneath that magnificent coat of colors as it had walked by him. He had felt such a love for that tiger. He remembered thinking at that time that he just wanted to reach out and to open the cage door to free that proud, regal being from its imprisonment, to let it be free to roam as it wanted. The second memory came quickly. As a child, he had read Rudyard Kipling's novel, *The Jungle Book*, about the young boy who is raised in the jungles of India by the wolves. The young boy had a special friend named Shere Khan, a large tiger.

The tiger reached them and stood there. Joey and Leigh felt an overwhelming urge to kneel down before him. As they did so, they noticed that everyone else in their group was also kneeling down. The tiger stepped close. Standing directly in front of Joey and Leigh, he was staring at them with deep eyes that had an ancient wisdom flowing from them.

Joey and Leigh were again given a subconscious urge, this time to reach out and to touch the tiger's head. As their hands touched the soft fur and began to stroke him, Joey heard and felt a deep rumble that seemed to vibrate from the very earth beneath their knees. This deep, rumbling sound was pulsating. Joey and Leigh felt an immense outflowing of love moving in both directions, from themselves toward the tiger and from the tiger toward them. Then Joey recognized what that deep, rumbling sound was. It was the sound of the tiger purring.

All of them gradually became aware that they were now enveloped in a cloud of a misty white light. It was a warm vapor with a sweet scent of herbs in it. It was filled with such a powerful sense of love. Joey and Leigh found themselves gradually filling up with a deep sense of awareness of other things and of other ways of seeing what was around themselves, an opening up of their minds to other things. They began to lose their sense of where they were and when they were. They heard a low murmur of a deep voice saying something to them, almost as if from a great distance. It gradually came closer. It slowly began to become clearer to them. It was a deep male voice, full of serenity and peace. To their surprise, it was speaking words to them—not verbally, but within their minds.

Their awakening took another big step upward when they realized that the voice that was talking to them was coming from the tiger. He was speaking to them telepathically, "Hello, Joey. Hello, Leigh. I am Dama. I am an ancient being by your years. I have been in existence for more than one hundred thousand of your Earth years. I have been hoping to meet you both, and now you are here. I am so happy to see you both. The Great Spirit, that supreme power that guides us all—it has arranged for us to meet at this time and this place. Both of your paths are moving into a new phase of your lives. You both are destined to become very important people for your world. You three are to be the message carriers from the Great Spirit and from me to your world."

Joey and Leigh had the same thought at the same time: *What did he mean by us three?* Dama almost smiled. He then stepped closer to Leigh, and he placed both of his front feet onto her, his left one on her left shoulder and his right one on her abdomen. Leigh froze in place. There was no sound, no fear, no sense of danger, just an overpowering sense of some strong connection taking place.

After a few moments of what seemed like an intense quiet, Dama brought his front feet down and moved back a few feet. Leigh had a strange look on her face. She turned to Joey, and they looked into each other's eyes. Joey was stunned. He saw Leigh and something else looking out at him from Leigh's eyes. Leigh and another.

Then Dama spoke to him again, "Joey, this new being that is growing within Leigh is a girl-child. She is destined to be my representative on your world. She is very strong now, and she will become stronger after her birth. She will lead the way for your world to turn to its Path of Peace. I have named her Naragoro."

Joey and Leigh were again washed over with a sense of universal love for all.

Dama's voice spoke to them again, "What was meant to be is now. Joey, Leigh, we four are now connected for all time. I will speak to you and you to me whenever you wish. The same for Naragoro. My people do not know time or distance. Whenever you wish to speak to me, just do so through your thoughts. Wherever any of you three are, so am I."

Dama stepped backward a few feet. Looking at them, he again seemed to smile that oh so gentle and loving smile. "I welcome you both to this part of your path. The changes that are happening are very powerful, and you are going to be amazed at what's coming up for you both. I can see ahead, but I cannot tell you what is coming for you. If you knew ahead of time, then it might change the outcome. I wish you three a long, happy, joyful path.

"Yes. There will be times of turmoil, but you are on the right path for you and your world. Eventually, we will meet face to face again, maybe at that time when we all stand in front of the Great Spirit."

Dama turned away and began to walk back toward the buildings. As he did, the gentle white mist that had been around them all started to clear up. Almost as if they had all been in a trance, they all started to look around and then started to slowly stand up. Looking at one another, they all saw that this experience had been one that was shared by them all. There was a mutual silence, as if no one wanted to be the first to break this peaceful, reverent moment.

Arnor motioned with his right arm that they should start back to the shuttle. The silent group walked slowly toward the landing area, with everyone in deep, contemplative thoughts about what they had just experienced. As they reached the shuttle, Joey glanced at Arnor and saw him looking around at the mountain ridges near them. He suddenly had a surprised look on his face. Joey turned to look in that direction. What he saw also surprised him. The sun was setting behind the low ridge. It had been late morning when they had arrived here. Their encounter with Dama had lasted for more than eight hours. They had lost all sense of time while they were speaking with him. Somehow, they had all been in a kneeling position and conversing with this powerful being for eight hours and not knowing or feeling the passage of time.

They all stepped back into the shuttle and sat down.

CHAPTER TWENTY

As they were sitting down in their seats, Arnor took the pilot's chair and called back to Joey, "Joey, would you please come up here and take the copilot's chair?"

"Sure, Captain Arnor." Joey went forward and sat down.

Arnor activated the power systems. They slowly rose upward and started to move forward back across the valley toward the home of Savak's family.

The ride was quiet. Everyone was still in their own deep, contemplative mood. About halfway there, Arnor turned to Joey and said, "Well, it's about time you started to learn some new things. It's now time to learn about some nighttime flying. Put your hands on the controls just the way my hands are. I will guide you in how to handle one of these shuttlecrafts. These screens are for sensors. Here is your direction and speed."

After about an hour of quiet riding, Joey was still amazed by the lack of engine noise.

Arnor quietly started to talk to him, "What happened back there with Dama, that was what I hoped would happen. When I went to your world to find you and Leigh, Dama asked me to try to get you here to see him. This meeting was meant to be. I am so grateful for this.

"Now, please listen to me carefully! This may be the only chance that I get to teach you these things on this world. Here, we also see it as having an up and down. We say *upper world* or *lower world*. If you look out at the mountain ridgeline there, off your right shoulder. Can you see it? Yes, right there. That bright star is where we look when we are trying to see the upper-world direction. Now keep that on your right shoulder for about one more hour, and we will be near Savak's family home."

Joey was listening closely. Flying this machine was so wonderful for him. On Earth, he had considered taking flying lessons. But this was so much more than putting around in a Piper Cub while making a lot of noise. He glanced over his left shoulder, back into the seats behind himself. He saw that everyone had drifted off to sleep. Leigh looked so beautiful there. *God, how I love her,* he thought. Savak and Mara were folded together like some kind of modern sculpture, both of them very much asleep. Even Bara was snoring slightly. Looking back at Arnor, he found him looking around and perhaps thinking similar thoughts.

Speaking quietly so as to not wake the others, he said, "I have had dreams for some time now that included a tiger in them. Now I think that I know why. This is a great chore that Dama has asked us to do. But we will give it our best. I am still in awe of how he was able to place us in that dream state for eight hours while he talked to us. He has such power. And he uses it for peace. What a wonderful being he is."

Arnor murmured, "Yes. And he has been this way since he came to our world that many thousands of years ago. You are going to find that this connection that he spoke of now extends to all of us who were there today. We are all now joined together on this spiritual plane. Do not be surprised that each of us had our own message from him. You and Leigh have yours. I have mine. Savak and Mara have theirs, and Bara has his. This is one of the ways that Dama works with us all."

They were quiet again, deep within their own thoughts.

About an hour later, Joey saw lights in the distance up against the side of a dark mass that he now knew to be a mountain. Motioning to Arnor, he pointed. Arnor motioned to him that he would take over the controls for the landing because it was nighttime.

A short time later, they came in to the landing area and set down quietly. The mild thump woke up the others. Everyone stood up and exited the shuttlecraft. There seemed to be a spur-of-the-moment need for everyone to reach out and hug one another, like friends who have shared a major life-changing experience. Then they all headed off to bed and some rest.

As Joey and Leigh were climbing into their bed, he looked at her and asked, "Are you OK?"

She looked into his eyes and smiled. "I love you, my huckleberry friend. Yes, I am fine. I have such a warm glow of peace within me right now. I have never felt this good in my life. He gave us something very special. I now know that we are going to be all right for the rest of our lives. This new path that we have been placed on is like nothing else that we have ever known."

They started to drift off to a deep sleep, when they heard, on a very deep level within their minds, a deep, pulsating rumble, like what a large cat would make when it purrs.

Waking up in the morning became a slow, gentle process. Joey glanced out of the window and was surprised that it was almost midmorning. They had been so tired when they got to bed that they had overslept. The rest of the area of the building that they were in was being kept quiet for the guests who had been late in returning last night.

After getting cleaned up and into clean clothes, they headed out into the compound. Leigh was wearing one of her new dresses. The ship's crew gathered together in a dining area of the main building. There were just those people of the ship's crew here for this late brunch. The small talk was like that of a group of very close, special friends. Arnor asked them if they wanted to join Joey and Leigh when they meet with Metaron a little later. But he also told them that they had to start getting ready for the return trip to the *Universal Peace*. There was one more world for Joey and Leigh to stop at. Then the long journey back to Earth. Everyone agreed to be with Joey and Leigh for their meeting.

They gathered in an outdoor garden area surrounded by flowers and flowering shrubs, with the bright-blue sky and the warm sun. A gentle breeze stirred the air.

Metaron was sitting on a stone bench when they arrived. He looked at the group and burst out laughing. "Come, come. Please sit here near me. It's such a beautiful day I thought that we should be here in the sunshine, this wonderful gift from our world's goddess."

Reaching out to Leigh as everyone was sitting down, he touched and held her hands. "Yes, yes, I was told in my dreams. You are the one that he has chosen. I am so happy to have met you both. He has placed such a hopeful task with you both. But you will have a lot of help, some of it from very unexpected sources."

He burst out into a joyful laugh again. Turning to Savak and Mara, he reached out and held Mara's hands. Speaking softly, he said, "Mara, you both are to have a part to play in all of this. I also see a long togetherness for you both. And you will be gifted with young. There will be two of them. Oh, I see such joy for you both!

"To you all, remember that for all of you, your paths are now intertwined. This is a great spiritual path that you share."

They sat in the sunshine and chatted for a while more.

Then Metaron said, "Now you all have to go back to your home in the sky.

"Arnor, safe travels for you and all of those on *Universal Peace.*

"Savak, Mara, Dr. Bara, Joey, and you, Leigh, may you all walk a Path of Peace and beauty."

He stood up, and then everyone grouped together and shared hugs. The ship's crew turned and returned to the shuttle. They were met by a large group of Savak's family.

Mara's mother walked up to Leigh and placed her hands on Leigh's abdomen. She whispered to Leigh, "May you and your child be happy. You both have given us the wonderful gift of staying here at our home and sharing the ceremony of Savak and Mara's Life Partnership. We thank you all. Here is a gift for your child to give to her after she arrives. I also give my wish to you both that you may return here at some point to stay with us again."

Leigh was in tears. She hugged her, and they all entered the shuttle.

Two hours later, they listened to Arnor's familiar litany: "*Shuttle 4* to *Universal Peace. Shuttle 4* to *Universal Peace.* I am approaching the landing bay. Please open the door. Start making all preparations for getting underway. Navigation, make our next destination the world known as Therma."

"Yes, Captain Arnor. Make all preparations for getting underway. Our next stop is Therma."

Again, Joey was taken aback by the sudden appearance of the great square opening suddenly appearing in what looked like the middle of nowhere. The shuttle moved into its parking spot. The door slowly closed.

When the atmosphere was normalized, they exited the shuttle and headed off to their different quarters. Arnor handed his clothing bag to a crewman and headed to the bridge control station. There was the background bustle of activity that always signaled their getting-underway routine. Leigh and Joey headed to their quarters, Bara to his health-care station, Savak and Mara to their new shared quarters.

A short time later, Joey was headed to the engineering section. Again, his wrist communicator beeped. He switched his direction and headed to the bridge. Leigh changed into a loose-fitting dress and headed toward the health-care station.

When Joey arrived on the control bridge, Arnor motioned him to a chair beside himself. Joey sat down. Arnor spoke to him in a soft tone, but there was some sort of underlying sternness in it also. "Joey, I received permission to take you to a world named Therma. We are going to be underway for ten days to arrive there. Before we arrive, I want to sit down with you and Leigh. I need to explain why we are going to this dead world. But right now, I need to focus on getting us moving and into open space. I would like to have you start sitting next to our different operations stations to learn about them. Is that all right with you?"

"Yes, Sir. Where do you want me to start?"

"Thank you, Joey. Will you please step over to that left corner beside the view screen? You can start with our communications station."

For Leigh, it was simpler. Bara welcomed her into the health-care station and immediately asked her if he could do a routine examination on her. She was now just getting ready to start the third trimester of her pregnancy. He was concerned because of the amount of activity that she had been through recently. Leigh disrobed and sat up on the examining table.

Bara used one of his special tools. It looked like a small tube. It read and transmitted its findings into the health-care computer. He murmured to himself as he worked. Finally, he finished. Telling Leigh to put her clothes back on, he went to the computer and entered his report. Leigh finished dressing. Bara turned to her with a stern look on his face. She began to get worried. Suddenly, his face broke out into a wide grin.

"You are doing tremendous. I was worried about all of the activity that you have had lately, but you are great."

Leigh gave a sigh of relief.

Bara continued, "I am going to try to keep you from being exposed to any of the diseases on board, if I can. Injuries, yes. Diseases, no. And I'm going to get someone else here to help us with anything that requires lifting, although our tools work very well with those problems. I am not used to having a pregnant woman on board, so I'm a little nervous about having anything happen to you."

Leigh smiled and said, "Don't worry, Dr. Bara. I've had experience with this before. I know how to act."

Later, she and Joey were joking about it all.

Nine days later, and they were approaching the world of Therma. Arnor had been quiet about it all. He was waiting until they had arrived before he talked to Joey and Leigh. Now *Universal Peace* was slowing and passing by the sun of this system and toward a world that looked to be a little smaller than Earth. But Joey thought that it had an unusual look to it. Something was not quite right. Arnor was watching him looking at it. Joey thought that the color was almost a dusty tan. He could see no blue. Everything was blurred. Nothing could be seen clearly.

Arnor spoke quietly to Joey with sadness in his voice, "Joey, this world is a dead planet. There is no life at all here. Everything here is dead. This planet's culture killed itself and the planet with it. That's why we are here now. So that you can see what this looks like."

CHAPTER TWENTY-ONE

Universal Peace slowly maneuvered into a stationary orbit over this world known as Therma. The magnification systems showed a world that looked like a huge dust bowl. The only colors that could be seen were a mix of tans and browns, broken by the blackness of rock. No water was visible on the surface.

Arnor stood up. Speaking into the communications system, he said, "Captain Arnor to the landing bay. Please ready a shuttle. Myself and a small crew are going to visit the surface of this world for a little look-see."

"Landing bay to Captain Arnor. Yes, Sir. We are preparing a shuttle now, Captain. And we are adding the extra protection systems needed for this world, Sir."

Arnor spoke to the bridge crew, "I will be taking Mr. Savak, Joey, Leigh, and Dr. Bara with me. Mr. Chara, you have the conn. We are not, I repeat, not going to touch the surface. We are going to be conducting a slow scanning trip."

"Yes, Sir, Captain. I have the conn."

One of the bridge crew stood up and walked over to the captain's chair and faced the doorway leading from the bridge. Joey had worked with this man just a little, but they were growing to be friends. Despite this man's appearance, he was a friendly person and very good at his work. Mr. Chara was one of the members of that species who looked just like a large grizzly bear.

A short time later, they were all on board the shuttle and moving slowly toward the planet's surface.

Arnor began a narration about this world: "This is a new experience for you and Leigh, Joey. But everyone else has been here before, some of us many times. Our Worlds Administration makes this place a mandatory stop for all ship's crew members. They are all shown this world as a lesson in what can happen.

"Therma was once, about thirty thousand of your Earth years ago, a planet with an active species. They had grown to inhabit the whole planet, and they were starting to reach out to other worlds near themselves. We had been watching them for some time. They were like some other worlds that we have encountered, self-centered. They were always carrying on some type of warfare. All of their various administrations were full of greed. All that they wanted to practice was hate, fear, violence, and suppression of anyone that spoke up against themselves. They were more focused on weapons than on health. They had scoured their planet of most of its natural resources. Greed for wealth and power was the ruling intention of their leadership.

"We knew from our experience where their path was taking them. We reached out and contacted a few of them in an attempt to start changes in their culture. We were hoping we could get them to make the changes before their ecology reached its collapse point. We knew that once that happened, well, then it was all over for their world."

The shuttle was, by now, slowly cruising over the surface at a height of five hundred feet. Joey was stunned at the devastation that he saw everywhere. Everything was a dry, sandy surface. Even the rocks were dried out. Joey was reminded of the pictures that he had seen of the planet Mars. No water or even the signs of water were visible. There was an intermittent wind that was blowing the dust and sand into small whirlwinds. But this staggering scene had no signs of anything green at all. No plants. Not even any mosses. The very air itself seemed to be colored with a slightly reddish or pink tint. It didn't even look healthy. It looked more like some sort of huge hazardous material spill.

Mr. Savak, who, in his official capacity, was *Universal Peace*'s science officer, was intently studying his scanning instruments. He interjected, "Captain, my scans are now showing a slight amount of moisture in the air, less than 1 percent by volume. I am also showing a less than 1 percent amount of oxygen in the air. Sir, there is not enough of either to sustain life. But, Sir, I am also showing a slight increase of these things over my last scanning from here on this planet. There may be a slight hope for this world's future. Perhaps in five hundred years, it may be able to support life again."

Arnor spoke again, "We had decided to isolate this world from the others in the nearby systems to prevent the spread of their blackness, their greed, and their hate. Then we just moved back a little and watched carefully. It took about fifty years, but when it happened, it was sudden and catastrophic. Each world is different. But they all share the same traits. If their world's natural systems are abused enough, they reach that pinnacle when it all collapses. And once the collapse starts, then it's too late for anyone to say 'I want to change my mind.' The collapse starts, and they only can watch as the planet and everything on it die. For this world, the abuse continued until that day when the water, soil, and air became so polluted that they became poisonous to all life forms. It all collapsed then. Within just three or four years, all life here had ceased to exist: plant life, water life, animal life. Everything died. We could do nothing. We waited for a few more years, and then we came back in close to scan the surface, to check for any survivors. There was nothing left.

"Since that time, we have used this world as a training tool for other peoples that we have contacted. We bring certain members here and show them what can happen to worlds that choose to ignore the messages and signs of their downfall. Joey, your world, Earth, is on this path.

"We—myself, Dama, Metaron, the other leaders that we have— are hoping that with our help, you and Leigh can return to your world and spread our messages to make them change their path."

Joey heard a deep sadness in his voice. No one likes to witness such a loss as this must have been.

The shuttle continued its slow travel over the world's surface. By this time, even the buildings' ruins had disappeared. Nothing. Nothing remained of whatever people and culture had once occupied this planet.

After a short while, there was a silent communication among everyone. They had seen enough. Arnor adjusted the shuttle controls. They began to ascend back upward toward their orbiting home. No one had anything to add. The silence said it all.

The return to the *Universal Peace* and its landing bay was quiet once back on board. When they were able to exit the shuttlecraft, Arnor started giving instructions for getting underway again.

"Captain Arnor to bridge. Make all preparations for getting underway. Our next stop is the world known as Earth. I will be on the bridge in a few moments."

"Bridge to Captain Arnor. Make all preparations for getting underway. Our next destination is the world known as Earth.

"Bridge to Captain Arnor. We are making preparations for getting underway."

Turning to Joey and Leigh, he said, "Well, now we head back to your world. This part of our journey will take us about 110 days. We have some things to chat about, especially between those of us who met with Dama. He has given us a challenge to work on. But we can do this if we work together as a team. We have been given a special, powerful bond between us."

Back in their quarters, Joey and Leigh changed into work clothes and went to their respective areas. Leigh joined Dr. Bara in the health-care station. He took one look at her face and left her alone to her thoughts.

Joey went to the bridge. This time, he was offered a chance to work with Mr. Chara, as he supervised the protective systems for the ship. Chara began to quietly explain to him the differences among the detector systems, the deflector systems, and their weapons systems. He explained that these were used only in case they were attacked by something but that they also could be used if they were threatened by a meteorite that was able to get past their deflectors. The weapons systems were all based on the laser-type devices.

That evening at dinner, Leigh voiced a concern that she had. "Joey, if it is going to take them 110 days to reach Earth, well, there might be a problem. My pregnancy is due to be completed in about 75 days from now. This means that I would be giving birth on *Universal Peace*. This could create some problems. Dr. Bara is a great doctor. But he had never delivered an Earth human baby before. And there were no handy-dandy textbooks to help him to study for this."

Joey was bothered by this. This meant that only he and Leigh had had any training in this at all. His was because he had been an emergency medical technician working on rescue units. And Leigh would be the patient when that time came. He thought this over for a few minutes. Then speaking to Leigh, he suggested, "Honey, what if I assisted at the delivery? And what if you started teaching Dr. Bara about human births now? Would that give us enough time to get ready?"

Leigh thought on this and replied, "That might work. Yes, let's try that plan. Thanks, hon."

The next few weeks were a time for them to return to the ship's normal schedule. Arnor was even including Joey in that schedule of working so many days and having a few days off to do as he pleased. Leigh was slowing down on her work to give herself time to get some rest. She told Joey that it was a standard joke between her and Dr. Bara that now she was the teacher and he was the student. He was thoroughly enjoying learning about Earth human–birthing techniques.

They had been underway toward Earth for about six weeks. Joey was on his scheduled days off. He walked to the landing bay area in the hopes that he would be allowed to spend some time inside one of the shuttles. He wanted to sit in the captain's seat and go over the controls. He felt that spending some extra time doing this would help him remember them better.

Entering the open broad main floor of the landing bay area, he said hi to the shop supervisor. Telling him where he was headed, Joey started to walk across the floor toward his faithful steed, *Shuttle 4*. Walking around the stern end and heading toward the bow, he saw an engineer crewman pick up a handful of tools from a tool cart that was standing just outside the door to the shuttle. Joey walked to the door and peeked inside. He heard voices coming from the shuttle control cabin. Stepping inside and turning to the left, he walked to the cabin area.

Joey saw two engineers there. One man was on the floor with his head and shoulders inside the main control console cabinet. The other man was helping him by handing him the tools that he asked for and telling him what needed to be done. Joey was surprised and a little happy when he saw whom the second man was. It was Jaco.

"Hey, Jaco. How are you, man? I haven't had the chance to see you lately. I've been working on the bridge all the time."

Jaco turned and smiled. "Hi, Joey. Hey, what are you doing here? This is a long way from the bridge."

"Listen, man. My family told me what you did for them. I want to thank you so much for that. It made them feel so much better."

Joey just shrugged his shoulders. "No problem, man. It's just what I do. So, what are you two doing here anyway? Is there a bad problem? Is there something that I can do to help?"

Jaco said with a small smile on his face, "We have a control console signal box that's acting like it's really tired. We are trying to remove it and put in a new one. But this old one is jammed into position. And a cross brace is stuck in position. It's pretending to be an Earth human and being very stubborn."

Joey chuckled at the workman humor. "Well, I have personal experience with that problem."

It was something that he really enjoyed. He started to step forward to help, when the engineer on the floor suddenly grabbed hold of the tool that he had pushed into the small space behind the console signal box. He had braced his feet against the nearby seat support. He gave a grunt and heaved with all his strength.

From that instant on, everything would become a blur. Joey, for the rest of his life, as much as he tried, would not be able to remember all what happened next. Parts of it would remain forever as scattered bits and pieces floating around in his memory.

He would remember seeing that bright arc of electric power entering the crewman's left hand and exiting him at his right shoulder, the man's body, in its, oh so rigid arc, as all his muscles contracted in a heavy spasm. He would remember seeing the burned black hole at the man's right shoulder, seeing the smoke pushing forth from the charred skin.

CHAPTER TWENTY-TWO

The control box had broken loose from its framework, and with its maze of attached wires, it had fallen downward onto the workman's left arm. The tremendous electrical short, through the man's body. The noise was a muffled grunt mixed with a scream that was cut very short. There was that double flash of a yellowish-bright-white light. Joey would remember the flash at the left hand of the crewman. Later, they would find that the crewman's hand had burned off. The second one at the man's right shoulder, as it was jammed against the cabinet framework, had left a baseball-sized hole into the shoulder. It had burned through the muscles and deep into the very bones.

Joey had instinctively looked away from the flash of light. Then he raised his eyes to look out the view screen of the shuttle. That was when he saw that the electrical short had started the shuttle's propulsion system. The shuttle had lifted slightly and flown forward in a leap of speed.

Joey and Jaco were thrown backward by the movement. Joey grabbed at the copilot's seat. He did not see just where Jaco had landed.

Joey would forever remember his next view. The shuttle crashed into the huge landing bay doors. Joey watched as the impact shattered the shuttle's view screen, leaving a man-sized hole in the front of the shuttle. At the same moment, the impact had buckled the landing bay doors outward, leaving a gaping large hole in the hull of the ship.

Joey stood there looking outward at open space. It was just four feet in front of his arms, with nothing between him and the open space except outward rushing air.

Joey felt that push of air rushing past him and trying to carry him with it as it flew outward into the space. He instinctively used his arms to brace himself against the force of that air leaving the shuttle. Then he took an instinctive breath, and the nightmare took another step upward. There was no breathable air now. The air in the shuttle had all rushed outward into vacuum. He was experiencing that ancient nightmare of all living species: being unable to breathe.

Joey tried again to take a breath. Nothing was there to breathe. He started to feel that darkness coming on, that circle of darkness that crowds in around your eyes when you are losing consciousness.

A strong hand was pulling at his left shoulder, roughly pulling at him, forcing him to turn around. He was losing his strength rapidly.

Suddenly, a rough hand was forcing something over his lower face. Something with a rubbery feeling was being forced over his mouth and nose. He started to fight it, but the rough hand was stronger than he was. It was pushing something onto his face now.

He heard a slight hissing noise. In his panic, he tried to take another breath. Oh, the joy. A miracle. His throat and lungs were suddenly filled with that oxygen-enriched air that he craved so badly. He took another and then another deep breath. His consciousness was rapidly returning. His awareness was coming back. He grabbed at the air mask that was being held at his face. Turning around, he looked for the reason for his lifesaving help.

Jaco stood just behind him. He held two ship's survival suits in his arms. He furiously pushed one of them at Joey's chest. His intention was clear.

"Get into this suit now if you want to live through the next few minutes."

Joey had never worn one of the suits before. He started to fumble to get it on. Jaco shook his head in frustration at him. He reached over to help Joey. The temperature in the shuttle was falling fast. It was already well below freezing. They both rapidly got into the suits. Once Joey was in his, Jaco reached over and picked up the helmet. Placing it down over Joey's head and giving it a quarter-turn twist to lock it in place, he nodded his head in approval. Jaco then finished getting himself dressed and put his own helmet on.

Joey looked at Jaco. He saw that his mouth was moving, but no sounds came to him. He shrugged his shoulders. Jaco smiled slightly, and picking up both of Joey's hands, he showed him how to tip forward the suit's control panel that was attached to the front of the suit. He showed Joey which panel dial to press "...cations now, Joey. The other push points are easy. The suit's heater comes on automatically. That red light on your heads-up display is the atmosphere indicator. Can you hear me now OK, Joey?"

"Yes, I can now. What the hell happened?"

"My crewman accidently caused a major short circuit in the shuttle's control console. It triggered the shuttle's propulsion system. We crashed into the landing bay doors. They have been breached. We are lucky. If the impact had been just a little harder, we would have ended up in space, floating away from the ship. We would have died quickly."

Joey turned and started to reach for the crewman.

Jaco stopped him. "He is dead. He died when the short circuit went through his body. We have to leave here right now and get outside of the shuttle. We have to get to the landing bay office now. This whole area is rapidly losing all of its atmosphere."

Joey became aware that there was a loud, blaring, pulsating noise coming from outside the shuttle. He nodded his head. They both turned and exited the shuttle.

They saw a few dozen figures running toward them from the office doors. They were still a few hundred feet away. A few of them wore special clothing, indicating that they were members of the ship's rescue crew.

Joey's mind kicked into emergency-responder mode. He grabbed at Jaco's shoulder and turned him around. The damage to the ship's hull was about the size of an average man. The atmosphere within the landing bay was still leaking outward. He looked around the area and saw what he hoped might work to stop the problem.

Pulling at Jaco's shoulder, he started to run toward a spot on a nearby wall. He reached the point on the nearby wall. Then pulling at the door of the emergency fire locker, Joey opened it and saw what he was looking for.

"Hurry, Jaco. Help me with this. When I get this stretched out, I'll signal you, and I want you to open the water valve here in this cabinet. Will you do that?"

Jaco was puzzled. But he nodded his head.

Joey pulled on the fire hose, and as it tumbled out of the cabinet, he moved back toward the side of the shuttle and the collision scene. He signaled Jaco to open the valve. The stream of water gushed forth from the fire hose nozzle. Joey aimed it to hit the wall just above the breach in the wall of the ship's hull. He watched and saw what he had hoped for as it worked its magic. As the water stream hit the deeply frozen surface of the hull and the shuttle, it quickly began to freeze into a very large patch of ice. It quickly began to close the opening in the hull.

The onrushing crewmen stopped and looked on in awe. They had never considered this as a solution. They watched as Joey aimed the water stream over the area until the breach was sealed again.

Joey waited a few more moments, and he signaled to Jaco to shut off the valve. They walked over to each other and just stood there.

They quickly were surrounded by the other crewmen. The ship's rescue crew came up to them pulling along suspensor stretchers, very firmly motioning them to sit down on the stretchers. They began to look them over for injuries.

The other crewmen were crowding into the shuttle to see just what had occurred.

Joey noticed a change in the heads-up display on his helmet. That persistent glowing red light suddenly began to twinkle a little. Then it changed to steady green. He reached up and began to remove his helmet. Looking over at the other stretcher, he saw Jaco doing the same thing.

The rescue crewman was standing next to him and watching him. Joey made a decision. He stood up. The rescue crewman started to put his hands on Joey's shoulders to push him back down onto the stretcher. Joey brushed his hands away forcefully. Joey turned and stepped over to where Jaco was sitting on his stretcher. When Joey stepped up beside him, Jaco just moved over a little. Joey sat down with him.

Jaco murmured, "You OK?"

"Yeah, how about you?"

"I'm all right."

Joey murmured, "Listen, man. I'd invite you out for a couple of cold beers, but I don't think that they have any on board."

"Yeah. That sounds like something that might taste good right now."

The initial hubbub was settling down now. The alarm had been shut off. The damage was being assessed. The emergency was over for now. The rescue crew came to Joey and Jaco. They said that they wanted to take them to the health-care station to be seen by the doctor. Joey and Jaco just sort of shrugged their shoulders. "Sure. Whatever."

Then the rescue crew told them that they had to be taken there on the stretchers. Joey and Jaco looked at each other and made a mutual decision.

Joey growled at them, "Nope. We're not riding there. We're walking there. And we walk together. Do you understand me?"

The rescue crewmen were astounded by this. But after looking at the faces of these two men, they stopped their protests.

Jaco and Joey stood up and carefully removed their survival suits, placing them carefully and gently onto the stretchers. They again surprised the rescue crew by folding them carefully, showing a great deal of respect for them. They both then reached out and patted the suits as a way of saying "Thank you for what you did for me."

One of the rescue crewmen grabbed Joey's arm and started to pull him toward the doorway. Joey angrily shook off the man's hand. He stubbornly stood his ground until Jaco stepped up beside him. Then the two of them, walking side by side, began to move toward the doorway. Two men who shared that special and powerful experience of having faced death while standing side by side together and with each other's mutual help had survived. That, oh so special, bond between people that many people never know of, that experience that grows into a brotherhood between people.

Jaco and Joey walked toward the doorway, and as they did, their hands reached out for each other. This was then their special brotherhood, of those who had met Death face to face and told him, "Come back later. I have other things that I want to do yet. And don't bother my friend either."

As they neared the doorway, there was a bustle of people coming out into the area. They saw Josa and Dr. Bara. They also saw Captain Arnor pushing his way past the crowd into the landing bay room. He saw them immediately and hurriedly moved toward them. They stood a few feet apart. Arnor looked at them both and saw that special look in their eyes, the difference that had grown between them. He knew what it meant. He too had been there once and had experienced it himself.

Smiling at them both, he said, "I'm told that you two have had an interesting time here. I am grateful that you both are OK. Accidents happen. If we can learn from them—well, that's what counts. You two go and get seen by the doctor. Then I want you both to take a few days off to get some rest. We can chat about what happened here later."

"Yeah. A very interesting time today."

Arnor stepped to one side. Joey and Jaco walked side by side straight ahead and out to the doorway. Arnor nodded his head in understanding.

CHAPTER TWENTY-THREE

When Joey reached the health-care station, the first person that he saw was Leigh. She had been called and told that an accident had happened in the landing bay area. There was a surprised look on her face. She watched as Joey and Jaco entered the station together. Joey smiled at her and nodded his head.

Everything was OK.

The look of relief on her face was enough.

It had been three weeks since the accident. Joey had been summoned to the captain's office. He and Jaco had been interviewed extensively. Arnor had made his report to the ship's headquarters office back on their home world.

Three days later, Joey and Jaco were again called to the captain's office. Arnor looked at them with his stern I'm-the-captain look on his face. Then he suddenly broke out into a broad smile.

"Jaco, Joey, you both are hereby awarded commendations for heroism for what you did. Joey, once more, I find myself thanking you. This is getting to be a habit. You have been right on both instances around this event. You told me some time ago that Jaco would become a valuable member of this crew. You were right. When the two of you sealed that breach in the ship's hull, well, you both deserve this award.

"Jaco, you are hereby returned to your rank as third engineering officer."

Jaco looked at Joey, and there were tears in his eyes. That bond between them was strengthened again.

A few days later, Joey and Leigh were walking on the crew rest area near one of the farming decks. As they walked along one of the pathways toward one of the ponds, they saw benches set up to sit on and watch the water. They picked one and sat down. There were a few other strollers walking around the area. Leigh was within a few weeks of her delivery date. She had stopped working at the health-care station. Joey was finding himself spending most of his time with her. Just being near her made him feel better. They both had worked to train Dr. Bara in what was going to come next with this human pregnancy.

Joey had noticed that there seemed to be a steady stream of women crew members now who found some excuse to visit Leigh. They all wanted to be near her, and it seemed that at some point in their visits, they would slowly reach out and touch her abdomen. They were so enjoying having a woman with them who was going through that, oh so special, experience that only women can do, that wonderful experience of being able to bring a new life into being.

Joey and Leigh were just enjoying the scene before them: the pond, the trees and bushes, the gentle breeze blowing past them with its scents from the nearby flowers. The lighting was designed to simulate sunshine. That just felt good to them both. Sensing movement coming toward them, Joey looked to his left and saw Jaco walking their way. Joey motioned for him to sit on a bench beside them. Jaco sat down just a few feet away.

They all quietly chatted. A short time later, there was a pretty female crew member who was walking along the pathway. As she neared them, she looked at them and stopped for a moment as if she was in deep thought. She stepped off the pathway and sat down beside Jaco. He sat there quietly for a few minutes. He turned to her and began to chat with her.

Joey and Leigh looked on for a moment then turned back to each other. A look passed between them, but they remained silent. Hope springs eternal.

Ten minutes later, Jaco and the female crew member stood up. Jaco nodded to Joey. He and the female crewman both strolled away along the pathway, chatting quietly.

That evening at dinner, Joey and Leigh saw them again at another table having dinner together. They looked at each other and smiled. Over the next few weeks, Joey and Leigh saw them together frequently. They both noticed that Jaco was smiling and laughing a lot now. Yes, things were working out well.

It happened so fast when it finally came. The biggest surprise was that it was about a week early. Joey was awakened in the middle of the night by feeling Leigh's body as it stiffened outward in pain. He quickly noticed that there was a puddle of fluid in the bedding. He knew in an instant what was happening. He quickly got out of the bed and stood up, calling out loudly, "Computer, call the rescue team! I need them here. Leigh is in labor. Quickly! *Now, now, now!*"

Moments later, the team arrived. Moving Leigh onto a suspensor stretcher, they transported her to the health-care station. Dr. Bara was waiting for them. Hurrying Leigh inside and into the energy chamber, he and Joey started the preparations. Bara placed that special hood over the top of Leigh's head, and her pain went away instantly. Now her body began its natural process of giving birth. The contractions were almost continuous. This new life wanted out and into the world *now*. The contractions began to move the child downward through Leigh's body and through the birth canal.

Joey was holding her hand. She was doing the deep breathing exercises. Dr. Bara was watching her vagina. Suddenly, he stiffened upward, and with a surprised look on his face, he said, "Oh . . . Oh . . ."

He reached forward, and a moment later, his face broke out into an enormous smile. He held his hands upward slightly, and they held a brand-new born human baby. Then he started to look a little confused.

Joey instinctively knew what the problem was. Letting go of Leigh's hand, he moved toward where Bara was standing. Reaching over him to the nearby table, he picked up the sterile scissors, setting them down on the table beside her. His movements became rapid but purposeful. With one hand, he picked up the connected umbilical cord. With the other hand, he picked up a length of sterile surgical cord. He quickly tied two knots close together on the umbilical cord near the baby's abdomen. Then, grabbing the scissors again, he cut the cord. He then placed a sterile dressing around the small end of the now-severed cord at the baby's abdomen. Then quickly moving the baby to the table, he started to clean it up with warm water and sterile dressing materials.

Bara stayed with Leigh. Suddenly, the placenta sack oozed outward onto the table. Bara picked it up and carefully set it aside.

Joey finished cleaning up his new daughter, and holding the baby carefully in his arms, he moved over to stand beside Leigh. Placing the child in her arms, they both were in awe of what they were now involved in. Leigh opened up her gown and placed the baby's mouth on her breast. They were all rewarded with a small sound of instinctive sucking noises. Everything was going to be all right.

Suddenly, they all sensed something deep within their minds. They heard and felt a deep, rumbling sound that began to pulsate. They all looked off into the distance for a moment. The sound was made by an ancient being who currently resided in a large tiger's body. He was giving them all his message of happiness about the birth of the child.

Joey and Bara finished cleaning up Leigh and the area around her. They moved Leigh into a health-care station bed where she could rest. It had been an interesting night for them. They both sat down in chairs near the bed and watched as Leigh held the baby in her arms. Joey watched her and was so in love with them both.

They all slowly drifted off into a light sleep.

Much later, they were awakened by noises in the adjoining room. Bara stood up quickly. Turning, he opened the door. The next room was crowded with people.

He was surprised to see that it was late morning. He, Leigh, and Joey had been dozing for a few hours. Bara looked at everyone. In the sudden stillness of the room, he spoke, "OK, OK. I know why you are here. Now listen to me carefully. Leigh and the baby are fine. But they both need rest. I am going to let a *few* of you, at a time, in to visit with her. But, and I say, but each of you can only stay for a few minutes. She needs her rest. Do you all understand me?"

Everyone nodded their heads in agreement.

Joey and Bara worked together to check the baby and Leigh for any possible problems. Nothing. The relief was wonderful. Later that day, Leigh, being careful, slowly got out of bed and began to walk around. Joey was trying to make her stay in bed.

She just looked at him and smiled. "You aren't the only stubborn Earth human on this ship."

He shut his mouth and smiled back. God, he loved her so much.

Arnor came by to visit. With him was Savak and Mara. Mara and Leigh sat together and just shared that new-mother energy that was flowing from Leigh. Leigh carefully handed the baby to Mara to hold for a few minutes. Mara suddenly had tears in her eyes. Joey watched this all happen. He looked at Savak and saw something deep in his eyes. Joey would later tell Leigh that he would not be at all surprised if, in the near future, Mara would become a new mother herself.

The steady stream of women crew members coming by to visit became constant. Joey and Leigh began to visit the walking-path areas again. They were both surprised and deeply pleased when they noticed that Naragoro, even as an infant, was a child who would look you in the eye and hold that look for a while. She was already becoming a child who thought a lot about things. The purring sound became something that they all heard and felt.

It was starting to feel like Naragoro would, later in her life, be able to claim almost three thousand aunts and uncles. When she got a little older and started to play with other children, that will be something to watch.

Universal Peace was nearing that place called Earth. Joey was again spending some time on the bridge control station. Everyone there had begun to accept him as a valued crew member. Arnor was moving him more and more toward being a pilot.

Joey had asked him about the time difference when they reached home. It would be almost nine months' difference.

Arnor smiled a little and said, "I'll show you when we get there. Don't worry, Joey. This always works."

Three weeks had passed. Leigh was in her glory with Naragoro. They were everywhere on board. The scuttlebutt had begun to circulate among the crew that she and Joey would be leaving soon. Many of the crew had started to develop a problem with their eyes. Every time they saw Joey or Leigh, their eyes would start to tear up. They had all begun to accept Joey and Leigh as family.

CHAPTER TWENTY-FOUR

The bridge crew was watching the star systems closely now. *Universal Peace* was approaching the area of Earth's solar system. Arnor still had their ship at full cruising speed. He and Savak were talking together a lot. The conversations seemed to be very intense. As the science officer, Savak was being asked to make a decision about their plan to return to Earth at the same time as when they had picked up Joey and Leigh. It was a very fine-tuned, delicate maneuver. A mistake could send them into the Earth's sun, or it could cause them to miss the time deadline by years.

Joey sat with Savak and Arnor at the science station on the bridge. He listened as they explained about the coming maneuver.

Savak explained, "Joey, we have done this before, and each time, it has worked well. But there is a risk. What we have to do is to accelerate the ship to its top speed. We then aim ourselves at the Earth's sun. It is rotating in a right-hand direction. We have to fly as fast as we can toward it, and at the last moment, we have to turn and pass it as close as we can against its rotation. Once we are in its outer gravity field, we will be moving around it in a left-hand direction. This maneuver will cause us to start moving backward in time to this system. The delicate part of this maneuver will be in judging when to stop the maneuver so as to come out of it in the right time frame that we want to. If we stay too long, we will come out of it some years in the Earth's past. If we come out of it too soon, we will come out too soon and have to do it all over again. Our angle of approach will be very specific also."

Three days later, they began the process. Arnor and Savak stayed on the bridge control station. *Universal Peace* began to accelerate to its maximum speed. They were aimed at Earth's sun.

This was continued for two more days. They were now nearing the sun, headed straight for its center. Joey was getting nervous. He called Leigh on his wrist device. He told her to make sure that she and Naragoro were braced into a sitting position, preferably into a corner, so that they wouldn't be thrown sideways.

As they neared the sun, Arnor spoke to the ship's crew, "Captain to all hands. We are at our maneuvering point. All hands, brace yourselves for this event. Make all preparations for rapid turns. Make sure all loose items are secured.

"All hands. We are starting the maneuver *now*."

Arnor ordered the helm crewman to start his turn to the left. *Universal Peace* was made to start a very sharp turn. Even with the ship's gravity systems on full capacity, they all were forced toward their right sides by the turn. Immediately afterward, the ship was forced to turn back to a straight course as they started around the sun's outer gravity field. Joey was stunned by the effect on his vision and his hearing. Everything that he could see became blurry, like a photograph of a car at high speed. The voices of everyone became distorted. It sounded like they were all trying to speak through some sort of padded, coiled tube. Words started to become so distorted that he was having trouble understanding what was being said.

Savak started to hold up his hands with his fingers extended as he counted down to the time when they would pull out of the maneuver.

Seven . . . Everyone was focused on doing their work.

Six . . . The ship began to vibrate.

Five . . . Chara was holding onto his computer desk and showing a grimace on his face.

Four . . . Arnor was looking so intently at his screens that it seemed as if he were frozen in place.

Three . . . The vibration was getting worse.

Two . . . Savak was groaning with his effort to stay standing upright where he could see everything.

One . . . Joey thought that he was going to vomit any second.

Now Savak dropped his hands.

Captain Arnor yelled out, "Now, now, now!"

The helmsman turned the ship's control bar. *Universal Peace* gave out with a groan of her own, as if in relief from the stress on her framework. She twisted out into space away from the sun's gravity field. The distortions of sight and sound stopped immediately.

Arnor immediately ordered their speed reduced to one-quarter speed. Everyone was taking a moment to reorient their senses back to normal. Then they all started to look around at those people near them. The same question was being asked in everyone's mind: *I'm OK. Is everyone here OK?*

Savak sat down and began looking at his instruments intently. Arnor was watching him. This would be the moment when they found out just how close they had come to their target date.

After a few moments, Savak looked over at Captain Arnor and shook his head. Arnor was rocked back into his chair. Savak spoke up, "Captain, we missed our target date by four Earth days. We are four days late in our target date."

Arnor let out a sputter of relief, and he almost glared at Savak. His friend and ship's science officer had an odd, interesting, but sometimes infuriating sense of humor. Joey burst out laughing. The bridge crew all started to laugh in relaxation.

Joey wanted to add to the humor. He spoke up so that everyone could hear. "Captain Arnor, Savak, if we're four days late, do you think that I can get someone on this crew to help me to get my pickup truck started? It is an older truck now. And the battery is tired."

Everyone laughed again.

They had done it. They were back here at Earth within the time frame that they had tried for.

Arnor returned to his I'm-the-captain role. "All right, everyone. Let's get back to what we were doing. Joey, if you need help starting your pickup truck, well, I think that you will have to do that yourself. That technology is so old for us that only our ship's historian might even know what the terminology is.

"All right, everyone, let's get back to our work. We still have to move back near to Earth. We have two special people here who have to go back to their home.

"Helm, let's bring her around and head toward that third planet out. I want an orbit near to its moon."

Two days later, they eased into a parking orbit near Earth's moon. It seemed that most of the crew had acquired some sort of quick spreading infection that made them all somber and near to tears. The thought of losing two well-loved crew members was showing. Joey and Leigh were carefully sorting their belongings into piles of what they could take home and what they had to leave behind. Bara had asked Leigh to meet him in the health-care station for a last examination. He was almost crying when he was finishing up. Leigh snuffled and gave him a good example of that new Earth thing that she had taught the crew.

It was decided that they wait until the next morning to take them back to Earth. At dinner that evening, Joey and Leigh sat with the bridge crew at their favorite eating area on Deck 6. It seemed that the entire crew, except for those unfortunate enough to be on watch, were eating at the same time and the same place.

Arnor waited until they had finished eating. He stood up and spoke loudly to everyone there, "May I have your attention, please, everyone? Listen up, please. Tomorrow, we are going to have to take these two *Universal Peace* crew members down to that world's surface and to leave them there. I will let you all know that they have requested to be allowed back on board *Universal Peace* at some time in their future to work here again as crew members. They have been told that they will always be considered as crew members."

There was an uproar of applause from everyone, with many calls for "Let them stay now." There were even a few calls of "Let them stay here. I'll go in their place."

Arnor continued, "They have been given a special task to do on this world. Dama, Metaron, and our Combined Worlds leaders have asked them to do this thing. They will be back with us at a later time.

"I would ask you all to please come up here in an orderly fashion to give them your regards. Please form up a line starting here." He indicated a spot near their table.

The rush to be first almost caused a breakdown in the peace and love mind-set that they all practiced. Joey, Leigh, and Naragoro were encouraged to remain seated. They were there on this receiving line for over five hours. This time, the tears flowed freely. There were many people who practiced that thing they called hugs.

Later, when they were back in their quarters, they were in tears. This ship and its crew had come to mean so much to them. Not many Earth humans could claim to have a ship like *Universal Peace* and its entire crew as their extended families.

Sleep would be elusive tonight. All three of them tossed and turned that night away.

CHAPTER TWENTY-FIVE

Early morning after a sleepless night came hard. Joey and Leigh were up, dressed, and had Naragoro up, fed, and dressed. They had eaten in their quarters. The thought of facing their crew-member friends again this morning was just too much.

Their bags were packed. Leigh was taking the clothing that she had been given with her. They had changed back into their Earth clothing. Both of them were pleased that the clothes seemed to fit them a lot looser. It seemed that all this space-traveling experience had encouraged their bodies to lose a little weight.

Their doorway chimed.

"Door open," Leigh said.

In walked Savak and Mara.

Mara spoke up, "We have come to help you carry your things to the shuttle. What can we take for you?"

Joey indicated three bags. They all walked out of their quarters. Leigh stopped and looked back into it before the doorway closed. This had been home to them for almost ten months now. She was thinking, *Almost a year here. Will I ever see it again?*

They walked along and took the lifts to the landing bay. As they stepped into the bay, they were met by a crowd of over six hundred crew members. The cheering was deafening. Finally, Arnor motioned for it to stop. Joey and Leigh stood there, and in between their tears, they thanked the crew and promised to try to keep in touch. Waving to everyone, they turned and entered the shuttle.

As they were settling in, Joey spoke to Arnor, "Captain?"

"Yes, Joey."

"Captain, can I request one more crew member to ride down with us?"

"Yes, you can. I think that I know whom you are thinking of."

"Yes, Sir. I would like to have Jaco ride down with us."

Arnor stepped to the door of the shuttle and spoke to someone outside, "Jaco, you are being offered a chance to ride down with us. Would you like to?"

Before he had finished speaking, Jaco, who had been waiting outside, stepped into the shuttle and moved to sit down. Joey was so happy.

Savak took the pilot's chair. He nodded to Arnor, who nodded back in agreement. Savak said, "Joey, how would you like to join me here? I have need of a good copilot, and I have been told by a good source that you are one."

Joey blushed and stepped forward to the seat that was waiting for him. Sitting down, the two of them began the preparations for getting underway.

Savak called to the ship's control, "*Shuttle 3* to *Universal Peace*. We are cleared to get underway. All passengers are aboard. Please clear the landing bay and open the doors."

"*Universal Peace* to *Shuttle 3*. The landing bay has been cleared. You are OK to depart. The doors are coming open now. Please have a safe trip.

"Good luck. A safe journey. Until we meet again. From this bridge crew to Joey and Leigh."

Joey responded, "We thank you, and to the entire crew of *Universal Peace*, Leigh and I are looking forward to that time in the future when we can all be together again."

The doors opened up, and Savak moved the shuttle out into space. Once they had cleared the doors, he had Joey take the controls.

It was a quiet trip toward Earth. As they moved past the moon, Savak made sure to activate their shields to prevent their being seen.

Joey looked back into the shuttle. Mara and Leigh were almost huddled together. Mara was holding Naragoro. Joey was thinking that there is something truly wonderful about women holding and caring for a newborn baby. He had to remind himself that Naragoro was now almost a month old.

They were nearing the Earth's atmosphere. Savak took the shuttle's controls. He was slowing down to enter the thickening air.

Then they were moving over a vast, forested area in the northern half of the world. It was just before sunrise. It was cloudless and promised to be a beautiful day ahead.

Savak, finding the location that he was looking for, started to slowly spiral downward. Joey could not see any lights in the wide area that they were entering.

Then they were into the forested area and lowering down slowly into the trees. Savak knew exactly where he wanted to be. He brought them down to land beside a barely seen woods trail with a gentle bump. He gave a quiet murmur, "We're here."

They stood up and moved toward the doorway. Everyone stepped outside. The very early-morning light mixed with the scents of the forest. For a moment, Joey was sure that something was wrong. But he later realized that it was just the idea of being back here in this forest on this world that felt odd. He motioned to Jaco to walk with him. He sensed that this was the first time that Jaco had been here on Earth itself. Picking up their things, they started to walk along the trail back to the logging road. Savak stayed with Mara. She had never been on this world before either.

The light was starting to grow stronger now. They could see well ahead of themselves. Finding their way back along the logging road became a gentle walk. Joey was remembering that earlier walk that he and Leigh had made with this company.

After about twenty minutes, they were at the picnic-area clearing. There sat Joey's pickup truck. He slowly looked around. The only thing that he could see that was out of place was that a bear had tipped over the trash barrel and scattered the material all over the area before munching on Joey and Leigh's lunch leftovers.

He chuckled a little. It was just an old Earth reality check. This place was, after all, that bear's dining room. They saw nothing to put them on guard. Everyone walked across to the truck. This was the moment the he and Leigh had been dreading: the time to say good-bye to these special friends.

Fishing through his pockets, Joey found his truck keys. Opening the truck door, he saw that everything was all right. Placing their bags in the back of the truck, he struggled with his growing sadness.

Turning to face the crew, he and Leigh were almost sobbing. But this was part of the deal that they had made with Dama. He had told them that they would have times of turmoil. Suddenly, he felt that gentle purring sound in his head. Glancing at Leigh, he saw that she also felt this quiet message from their deep friend. Arnor, Savak, and Mara also smiled at the touch from their leader. Everything was going to be all right.

It happened so naturally. They all just came together in a large hug. Words were quietly mumbled. "Good-bye for now. We'll see you again later. Please keep in touch. Take care of yourselves. Please be safe. We'll be OK."

Stepping back a little, they all shared smiles, and then it was finished. Arnor, Savak, Mara turned and started to walk away back toward the old logging road. Jaco stood there for a moment more. He and Joey were looking into each other's eyes. Both were feeling the flow of tears down their faces. Then Jaco turned and strode off to join the other crewmen. As they moved out of sight, they each glanced over their shoulders for one last smile.

Joey and Leigh moved back to his truck. Sliding into it, they closed the doors and took a moment to compose themselves. Joey put the key into the ignition. The truck started right up. He smiled. It would take him a little while to recover from the time differences and other things. They fastened their seat belts. He backed the truck out of its parking spot and headed back toward the tar road. He and Leigh were quiet. Naragoro was nursing at Leigh's breast.

Later, on the road back past the Pines convenience store, he remembered that day when they had stopped here to get some sandwiches for a picnic lunch. He smiled when he thought that for the store owner, they were a nice couple that had stopped in four days ago. But now, for Joey and Leigh, they were now a threesome, and it had been almost a year.

They drove back down Route 27 through Stratton and North New Portland into Farmington, then onward southbound, down Route 4 through Livermore Falls, and then passed through Lewiston. Forty minutes later, they were back to their home outside of North Windham. They were reentering their old life again, but this time, they had been greatly changed. Their future was no longer an unknown. Now they had a task with its challenges: to try to raise Naragoro and to work with her to try to save this world that they lived on.

They arrived at their home, parked in the driveway, climbed down out of Joey's pickup truck, and they were presented with their first challenge. One of their close neighbors walked over to them to say hi.

"Hey, Joey. Hi, Leigh. You two were gone for a coupla days. I picked up your mail for ya. Hey, what ah you two doin' with a baby? Did ya adahpt it?"

Joey and Leigh took a deep breath. Well, this was going to take some creative shuffling of the facts. But the truth was not one of the options. These folks would not understand what had really happened to them.

"Hey, Walt. Thanks for getting our mail. Yeah. We met some friends in Eustis and stayed with them for a bit. Now we're back home again. Yeah. The baby is a gift that some friends gave us. We told them that we would help them out. She is really great. Hey, man. She is already sleeping all night through."

"Wow. That's great. Hey, I have ta get back ta tha house. Good ta have ya back home agin."

Joey and Leigh felt their muscles relax a little. Yep, this was going to take some adjusting to. But the future looked so awesome. They all heard in their minds that purring sound again coming from their ancient friend.

A short time later, as they sat on their patio and ate their lunch, they were rewarded with a scene like from a dream. They watched as Naragoro, sitting in her baby chair beside them, was visited by a stream of natural beings. First came a butterfly to land on her feet and to watch her. Then a bumblebee landed on her arm, followed by a dragonfly that stopped and sat on her chest; it seemed to want to stay with her for a while. Two chipmunks came by to play in front of her and to make her laugh out with joy. A squirrel with an acorn in its mouth came by to offer it as a gift. Joey looked across the road from their home and watched as two deer came to the edge of the trees and stood there watching them. He sensed a motion from above, just seen from the corner of his eyes. He looked upward and saw a bald eagle slowly circling around them and watching the area where Naragoro was laughing at her visitors. As if he was paying homage to this new messenger, there came again that rumbling, purring sound in their minds.

Yes, this was going to be an interesting time for them all.

Printed in the United States
By Bookmasters